MURDEROUS
MUMMY WARS

NICOLE ELLIS

1

———

"What are you looking at, Jill?" Desi Torres peeked her head around my office door.

I set down the photographs I was viewing at my desk and beckoned to my sister-in-law. "Come see."

She came over to me, her long skirt swirling around her ankles, and leaned over the desk to see them better. "Whoa. Is that a haunted house?"

I nodded and held up a handful of photos. "These are from when Angela Laveaux used to hold it in her garage."

Desi sat down in the chair opposite mine and took them from me. As she rifled through them, her eyes widened more with each one she looked at. "This was in her garage and yard? These are amazing!"

"I know. A few years ago, she moved it out to a bigger venue and the Ericksville Chamber of Commerce sponsored it. Your mom offered up the Boathouse for it this year, and I can't wait to see what she pulls off with all the space we have here." I laughed. "It might even make the past few months of dealing with Angela worth it to see what she comes up with." The heat kicked on and a draft from the ceiling air vent scattered the photos that Desi had discarded on the desk. I stacked them up neatly off to the side.

"Do you know what she has planned for this year?" Desi asked.

"Nope. Angela isn't the sharing type, and she hasn't yet divulged her plans to me." I glanced at my calendar. It was already the first of October. "She needs to do so soon though. Halloween is coming up quickly."

"Anthony and Mikey are going to have so much fun trick-or-treating this year. They're the perfect age for it." She made a face. "I love Halloween, but I'm not looking forward to the after-candy sugar rush. Four-year-old boys are active enough, even without the extra sugar."

"Adam is excited about taking them around our neighborhood this year with Tomàs, and he was thrilled when he heard we'd be hosting the haunted house. It's his favorite holiday."

"Yeah, tell me about it. When we were kids, he always had his costume idea ready in the summertime."

"This year is no different—except he's roped the kids and me into it as well. He wants Mikey and Ella to be Darth Vader and an Ewok, and for us to be Luke and Leia." I wrinkled my nose.

"But you hate *Star Wars*." She glanced up from the pictures.

"I know. But I couldn't tell him no. He looked so excited about the idea." Usually, I'd buy Mikey a costume at Costco or my mother-in-law, Beth, would make him one, but this year I was letting Adam take over costume duty. In the last three years, he'd only been home for one Halloween with Mikey, so I knew it was important to him.

"Well, at least you don't have to worry about it this year. I made Anthony a pirate costume this week and I didn't really think it through. As soon as I showed it to him, he took the rubber sword and ran off throughout the house, terrorizing the cat and knocking things off the shelves. We're now down two coffee mugs and an ugly vase we got for our wedding." She shrugged. "I guess some good things came of it. I hated that vase, but I didn't want to offend Aunt Arlene by sending it to the thrift shop." Desi lifted one of the photos and turned it around to face me. "Hey, did you see this one?"

The backyard of a grand old Victorian had been transformed into a creepy graveyard, complete with moss-covered tombstones and a freshly dug grave.

"Yeah. She went all out." I examined the historic home in the photo. I would guess it had been built shortly after Ericksville was founded in the late 1800s. "Her house is perfect for Halloween." The house was built of red brick and had some Gothic influences. A gabled roof extended high above the porch that spanned the whole front of the house. A wrought iron fence bordered the property.

"How did one person do all of this?" She handed the photos back to me. "These displays are pretty intricate. It would take me at least a year to put one of them together."

I shrugged and carefully filed them away in a photo storage box in order by year. Angela had loaned me the images to give me an idea of what the haunted house would look like, but I'd hate to think what she'd do to me if I lost any of them. "I think she had help setting it up, but as far as I know, the ideas were all hers. She's a local artist and Halloween is a passion of hers. She gets started months early with the plans."

Desi nodded. "I can tell."

I checked the clock on the wall. Four o'clock. Usually Desi was at the BeansTalk Café, her business located just down the block, at this time of day. What was she doing here so close to closing time? "What's up?"

She smiled at me. "Can't someone just visit their very favorite sister-in-law at work?"

I narrowed my eyes at her. "You want me to do something unpleasant, don't you? What is it this time?"

"I don't know what you mean," she said innocently. "I came here to ask if you'd like to go to a MUMs meeting with me. Nothing bad."

"A MUMs meeting?" The name rang a bell, and I racked my brain trying to remember where I'd heard it before.

"More United Mothers. You know, it's a group of moms who get together and do physical fitness and other activities together. Motherhood can be so isolating and the group's goal is to put an end to that. It's a national organization. A friend of mine told me about it."

I folded my arms in front of my chest and leaned back in my ergonomic chair. "Uh huh." With everything I had going on at the Boathouse, my husband's new business, and two small kids, I wasn't sure I had time to add something else to the mix. Plus, these groups had a way of needing way more of a time commitment than they initially let on.

"Jill! It'll be so much fun. They put you in groups with mothers of other kids born in the same school year as yours. Since Ella and Lina were both born last year, we can be in the same group. So cool, right?"

I smiled at her enthusiasm. "So cool." I was beginning to thaw to the idea, but I wanted to hear more about it before I made a commitment to Desi. If I told her I'd do it with her, she'd be crushed if it didn't work out.

"This group has more of a focus on fitness at the

4

moment as we're all moms who have had babies in the last year and we want to get back in shape. I've seen them out doing yoga in Lighthouse Park with their babies, and they go on easy local hikes with their babies in packs too."

"After what happened to Mikey last time we went hiking, I don't know if I want to go ever again."

She shook her head. "Mikey's fine. It was just an accident. He probably doesn't even remember it anymore."

"But I do." I was quiet for a moment. For Labor Day weekend, we'd gone on a family vacation to a lake cabin resort in Eastern Washington. On a nearby hike, Mikey had fallen off a steep edge of the trail. Luckily, we'd been able to pull him back to safety, but for at least twenty minutes, I'd been terrified. While our vacation had been fun, that was one of the memories from it that I'd happily never relive again.

"Anyway. Mikey wouldn't be with you for these meetings and you don't have to go on the hikes if you don't want to. All I'm asking is that you attend the meeting with me tonight. They have an interest meeting for new members at seven tonight in a conference room at the library. Moms only, no babies. I think there will be wine and snacks." She batted her eyelashes at me. "Pretty please?"

"I thought you said you had a friend that was already in MUMs. Can't you go with her?"

"Her youngest is two, so she wouldn't be in the same group. Please? Just try it one time with me and then if you don't want to go again, you don't have to."

"Are these all going to be stay-at-home moms that will make me feel guilty about going back to work?" I'd fought my own demons about that and I'd reached a good place in my life where I knew I'd made the right decision for me.

She sighed. "I'm sure there will be both stay-at-home

and work-outside-the-home moms there. The focus of the group is to unite moms, not create distance between them."

"Well, that's good to hear. I'm so sick of the whole Mommy Wars thing. What time did you say it was?" Although my husband Adam was home more now that he'd quit his demanding job as a corporate lawyer, I wanted to make sure he'd be able to watch the kids if I attended the meeting.

"Seven," she said brightly. "Adam can put the kids to bed and by the time you get home, you'll have free time. Win–win."

I looked at Desi. "Fine. I'll go with you and find out more about the group. But I'm letting you know now—if it doesn't work for my schedule, I won't be able to join. Right now, the haunted house is sucking up most of my time and energy."

"Understood." The metal legs of her chair skittered precariously on the hardwood floors before settling in an upright position when she stood abruptly. She circled my desk and wrapped her arms around me. "Thanks! I'd better get back to the café and help Andrea close up, but I'll see you tonight," she called over her shoulder as she hurried out of my office.

"See you." I sat back in my chair, surveying the mess on my desk. Photos, diagrams, and client paperwork covered the surface. A ceramic mug full of coffee fought for space near my computer. I took a whiff of it before setting it back down without drinking it—cold as ice. I hadn't even had time to drink my morning cup of coffee.

Maybe this MUMs group would be a good thing for me. Even though I'd vowed to not let work take over my life again, the haunted house had definitely disrupted the work/life balance I'd worked hard to cultivate since I became an event coordinator here last spring. It had been ages since I'd had a night out without Adam and the kids, and maybe I'd meet some new friends too. At the very worst, Desi and I could hang out, munch on snacks, and drink wine while finding out about the group.

2

       I pulled up to the library at ten to seven that night and turned off my car's engine, but didn't exit the vehicle. I didn't see Desi's car in the lot and I wasn't going in without her. At this time of day, things were winding down at the Ericksville Library, but a few stray people were still trickling in. A minivan similar to mine idled near the front door while a young boy jumped out and ran to the exterior book depository to return some borrowed items.

When the vehicle moved, I could see Desi standing next to the door, jabbering on her cell phone. I craned my neck around to check behind me. Sure enough, she'd parked on the opposite side of the library lot. I sighed. Part of me had hoped she'd change her mind about going, but now I was stuck.

I swung my purse onto my shoulder and gritted my teeth before opening my car door. A blast of chilly air hit me and I considered grabbing my jacket. As soon as September was over, the summer around here seemed to end abruptly and the days shortened dramatically. Soon, it would be dark by five o'clock and the winter rains would start. Who was I kidding? This was the Pacific Northwest. Once the rain started, it wouldn't stop until next May. I already missed the long summer days where we could sit outside on the deck until ten o'clock at night. I decided to leave my jacket behind because there was a good chance I'd forget it in the library if I brought it in. Besides, it was a short walk to the front door.

I slammed the car door and walked toward the library. Before I reached Desi, I took a long breath. *This could be good for you, Jill. It doesn't hurt to have more mommy friends.* Maybe this was what I needed as I navigated my way through the challenges of being a working mother of a preschooler and a baby.

"Hey," Desi said as she slipped her phone into her purse. "I didn't see you. Are you ready? This will be fun, I promise."

I had my doubts about that, but I smiled bravely and nodded.

Inside the conference room in the library's lobby, about ten to twelve women milled around, drinking wine out of plastic cups and eating cheese and crackers. Desi nudged me and winked.

"Told you there would be yummy snacks." She led me over to the refreshments table where we each grabbed something to eat and drink.

We stood together, waiting for the meeting to start.

"Hi, I don't think I've seen you two before. Are you thinking about joining our group?" asked a woman who was dressed in tight-fitting jeans and a flowered off-the-shoulder blouse.

Desi smiled. "Yes, a friend of mine recommended MUMs to me. She's in the class before this one." She gestured to me. "I'm Desi and this is my sister-in-law, Jill. We both have little girls under a year old."

"Oh, fabulous," the woman gushed. "I'm Lisa. I'm the

leader of our little group and we're just so glad to have you both here."

"We're glad to be here," said Desi.

I nodded my head. "Yes, it's great to be around other moms. I haven't been out without my kids in a while."

Lisa beamed at us. "You'll find we have a great selection of activities both with and without our little ones." A woman wearing a trendy long-sleeved knit shirt and designer jeans tapped her on the shoulder and muttered something in her ear. "Well, I've got to take care of this before the meeting starts, but please, mingle with the other women."

"We will, thank you." Desi turned to me. "This isn't so bad, right?" She peered at me with an anxious expression on her face. I knew this was important to her, so I vowed to make an effort to enjoy it.

"Nope, so far it's fine." I felt a little underdressed and disheveled in comparison to some of the other moms who wore perfectly applied makeup and obviously spent some time in the gym.

At the front of the room, someone clapped to get everyone's attention, and Lisa made her way there.

"Hi, everyone! I'm so excited to see our regular members and some new people too! If you could all find a seat, we're going to get started sharing what we have planned for our MUMs group for this year."

The group murmured as they sat down. Desi and I took seats next to each other near the rear of the room. I had a sinking feeling that this was a little like a PTA meeting. At the end of last school year, I'd daydreamed for a few minutes in a preschool PTA meeting and somehow ended up chairing the preschool auction. No way was that happening again. I straightened my spine and focused on Lisa.

"So, for those of you who don't know me, I'm Lisa Aldane." She waited as people said hi to her. "I have a three-year-old and a six-month-old, and I've been active in MUMs since my eldest was a baby. These have been some great years for me and I'm thrilled to give back as the leader for this group." She beamed at the audience. "We've got an outing to the zoo planned for next month and a stroller walking group that will meet three times a week. We'd love to have you attend. Also, we're going to be staffing the Ericksville Haunted House as a fundraiser."

Desi and I exchanged glances.

"Really?" she whispered.

I shrugged. This was the first I'd heard of it, but it wasn't really anything I needed to know about in my role as the event coordinator. All I knew was that Angela planned to take care of the staffing.

"I know all of you want to get involved, so we've opened up a few positions in our MUMs group. We're looking for a secretary and a treasurer for the year. They're both relatively easy and you'll report to the director of our local MUMs chapter. For the new people, this is a great way to meet people and be a part of our organization."

Desi's hand inched up. I shook my head in disbelief. She was crazy to want to add this responsibility on top of everything already on her plate.

"Desi, right?" Lisa said. "Are you interested in one of these roles?"

"I'd be willing to be the treasurer," Desi said. "I've done it before for the Ericksville Historical Society."

"Wonderful!" Lisa exclaimed. "So we've got our treasurer. Do we have any volunteers for the secretary position?"

Desi looked over at me.

I scrunched up my face. "No way."

Luckily, someone else volunteered before Desi could guilt me into it. Lisa continued on, talking about the group's planned activities, and the meeting was over by eight. I had to admit, it was nice to be out in the evening without the kids, even if it was in our local library. After most of the people had left, I hung back with Desi while she talked to Lisa about the treasurer position.

"So, there's not too much to it," Lisa said. "Here's our director's information and she'll get you all set up on our bank account and everything. I gave her assistant, Mindy, the books last time I saw her. I've been managing our funds since our last treasurer moved away, but I'm happy to let someone else do it now so that I can focus on my role as the leader of this group."

I snorted quietly. There was always more to these jobs than it seemed at first. Desi elbowed me and accepted the paper from Lisa.

"Thanks." She flashed a smile at Lisa. "I'll be sure to get in touch with her. Jill and I are looking forward to taking part in the stroller walk on Wednesday, right, Jill?" She eyed me.

I sighed. I did need to exercise more and this would force me to get outside and actually do it.

"Of course. It sounds fun." I looked around the room, where a few of the other moms were cleaning up. "Do you need any help?"

Lisa flapped her hand in the air. "Nope, we're good. Thanks again for coming." A movement off to the side caught her eye. "Oh sheesh, what is she doing?" She turned and stalked over to the table where an unsuspecting mom was unsuccessfully trying to stack plastic wine glasses on top of each other in a box.

Desi and I exited the library, stopping to chat outside. I shivered, wrapping my arms across my chest. This was where the jacket would have come in handy.

"So, what did you think?" Desi peered into my face.

"I thought it was uh ..." On the street behind us, a car drove past with its radio blasting, giving me a chance to consider her question. I wasn't sure what to say. While it could be good for me, I was already getting that sinking feeling in my chest like I'd committed to one thing too many. If everything stayed even, I could manage my workload, but that never seemed to be the case. As soon as I took on something else, Mikey would get sick or Ella would start waking up in the middle of the night again. With Beth's recent health problems, I didn't know if the status quo would change at the Boathouse, or if they'd need me to work more hours. I glanced at Desi. She looked so eager for me to join with her.

"You don't have to do it with me if you don't want to," she said in a disappointed voice.

I forced a smile. "No, it's fine. I'll try it out. We'll see how the first stroller walk goes, ok?"

A wide grin stretched across her face. "Thanks. I think you'll really like it. My friend just raves about her group."

"I'm sure I will. But I'd better get back to the house now. Hopefully Adam has Mikey in bed by now, but he sometimes loses track of time." We walked toward our cars, stopping next to hers.

"See you tomorrow." Desi slid into the front seat of her car and I walked back to mine.

When I arrived home, it was quiet, except for voices coming from the television. Adam must have successfully talked Mikey into going to bed. Lately, our son had developed a habit of procrastinating at bedtime. When the clock hit seven thirty, he suddenly realized that he was both extremely dehydrated and starving to death, and helpfully remembered all of the toys he'd "forgotten" to put away earlier.

"Hi, honey," Adam said from the couch as I came into the living room. He muted the TV as I walked over to him.

"No problem getting them to bed?"

"Nope. Mikey and I played outside for a bit after dinner and I think I wore him out." A self-satisfied smile appeared on his face. "He was asleep as soon as his head hit the pillow."

"Great." I plopped down on the couch next to him. "It's been a long day."

"Well, it's over now," he said. "Do you want to watch an episode of this with me?" He gestured to the TV.

I glanced at the screen. He was watching a rerun of his favorite sci-fi show, which he'd been binging on for the last few weeks. Not really my style. I had never seen the need for two televisions in our house, but now that Adam was home so much, I was having withdrawal symptoms from some of the junk TV I liked to watch—not that I wanted to admit my addiction to my husband. When he'd been gone almost every night, I had to have something to fill the long hours alone at night before I fell asleep.

"Nah, I think I'll head to bed soon. You can keep watching this."

He shrugged and aimed the remote at the TV to unmute it, but before hitting the mute button, he called over his shoulder, "Oh, you might notice that I moved some things around in the kitchen cupboards. I don't know how you ever found anything in there."

Great. I know I'd wished for Adam to be home more, but part of me was starting to regret that my wish had been granted. I walked with trepidation into the kitchen and opened up the cupboard that had held Mikey's plastic cups—a bottom shelf that I'd chosen so that he could reach them on his own. Adam had moved our heavy casserole dishes into the space. I hunted all over and finally found the cups in a top cupboard. I glanced at Adam, who was happily watching TV. Should I mention it to him now?

My phone vibrated insistently and I picked it up.

Desi: Call me now.

A discussion about the kitchen cupboards would have to wait.

"Adam," I said loudly to be heard over the television. "Desi wants me to call her. I'll talk to her upstairs so I don't bother you. Good night. Thanks for getting the kids to bed."

"No problem. 'Night." He absentmindedly turned back to the TV.

I hurried up the stairs and into our bedroom, closing the door behind me so I wouldn't wake the kids. I flopped on the bed and tapped Desi's name on my phone.

"Hey," I said when she answered.

"Oh my gosh. I just looked at the paper Lisa gave me with the name of the MUMs group director on it. You'll never believe who it is." She paused for dramatic effect.

I sighed. "Who?" As far as I knew, none of my friends or acquaintances were involved with the MUMs organization.

"Angela Laveaux," she said triumphantly.

My brain seemed to freeze. "What?" How could Angela be the director of MUMs? Then again, I didn't know her very well, and in all of our dealings, I'd never asked her what she did for a living. I guess I assumed she sold her art or something, but in all likelihood, that probably wouldn't cover the cost of living in the Seattle area.

"Well, that explains why the MUMs group is staffing the haunted house."

"Yep." She sighed. "I guess this means I'll be working with the infamous Angela now. With any luck, I won't have to deal with her very much. Lisa told me she has an assistant at the office who does most of the work."

"Lucky you. I wish I could say the same." I daydreamed for a moment about what it would be like to not have to work with Angela on the haunted house. It felt heavenly. I shook my head. Like it or not, I was stuck with her.

"So did you really like it?" she asked.

"I think it might be fun." I stretched out on the bed, suddenly as exhausted as Mikey had been.

"Good, I'm glad. Well, that was it. I just wanted to tell you about Angela."

I laughed. "It's funny how small a town this is. Good-night. I'll see you tomorrow, ok?"

"Yep. See you tomorrow."

The call disconnected and I forced myself to roll off the comfy mattress and go into the bathroom to get ready for bed. I'd finished brushing my teeth and dressing in my pajamas when I heard Ella cry out from down the hall. I didn't think Adam could hear her with the TV on, so I went to her room to rock her back to sleep. By the time I'd tucked her back into her crib, I was a walking zombie. I loved my little ones, but sometimes it seemed like a mother's work was never done.

Early the next morning, an alarm sounded. I rolled over and

smashed my hand down repeatedly on my nightstand, fumbling for my phone. When I finally was able to grab it and focus on the time, it read six thirty. The noise continued. That was odd—my alarm wasn't set to go off for another fifteen minutes and, after the late night up with Ella, I really needed the extra sleep.

I groaned. It wasn't my personal cell phone, it was my work phone—and it was ringing.

I picked it up and sighed. Angela Laveaux. Why was she calling me so early in the morning? The phone kept ringing in my hands. Finally, I answered. I didn't think she was going to give up.

"Oh, Jill, I'm glad I reached you." Her voice blared over the line, stinging my ears.

Adam asked sleepily, "Who's calling so early in the morning? Is something wrong?"

I patted his shoulder and held my hand over the receiver to mute it. "It's Angela. Go back to sleep."

Into the phone, I said, "Hi, Angela. Is there something I can do for you?" I slid my feet off the bed and stretched out my legs as she answered me. Our house was freezing. We turned the heat down at night and neither of us had turned it back up to our normal daytime temperature yet.

Goldie looked up at me from his doggy bed in the corner of our bedroom and I motioned for him to fetch my slippers for me. Like every other time I'd tried that move, he stared at me as if I were an idiot and lay back down.

On the other end of the phone, Angela prattled on. "We really need to get the decorations out of my storage shed today. If we don't do it today, we won't have enough time to get everything put together before the haunted house goes live."

I counted to five, and then said, "I think we still have

plenty of time to get everything together."

"No. I've been doing this for years and years, and I have my schedule down pat. We must begin now."

I could already tell this was going to be a long day. I did some mental calculations. We had reserved the main hall of the Boathouse for the haunted house for the next three weeks, so there wouldn't be any other events planned for that space. I could humor Angela and let her start moving her decorations in early. "That will be fine."

"Great. I'm going to need to have you come over and get everything from my shed. You do have people to do that right?"

I stared up at a paint splotch on the ceiling. In the off-season, we had less staff and there wasn't anyone available to help transport the Halloween decorations. I supposed it was up to me. Then a thought occurred to me. "Isn't the Ericksville chapter of MUMs planning on working the haunted house?

"Well, yes. I suppose they are." She was quiet for a moment. "I'll see if I can round anybody up to help you. I will be there, but my husband is highly asthmatic and he's not able to help move anything."

"Ok, keep me updated. I can come over today with a truck, but I won't be able to do it all by myself."

"Well, I guess that will just have to do."

Yes, it will, I said to myself. "Is there anything else I can do for you, Angela?"

"No. Not right now. I'll call you back if I think of anything." The phone clicked off and I slid back into the cozy warm sheets.

Next to me, Adam was awake and grinning. "Angela again?"

"Yeah."

He laughed. "At least you only have three more weeks of her, right?"

"Yeah. But that will be a long three weeks. I hope I don't have to deal with her next year." I brightened. "Maybe we can talk your mom into not hosting it next year."

"I don't think she'll take too much convincing," he said. "Mom seems pretty frustrated with her right about now. What all did she want you to do?"

"She wants me to move all of the haunted house decorations from her house to the Boathouse."

"Is that in your job description?" he teased.

I glared at him. He held up his hands, as if to ward off any attack from me. I could tell neither of us was going to get back to sleep, so I reluctantly forced myself out of bed and into an oversized fleecy bathrobe. "I should check on the kids."

"I'm going to take a shower, and then I'll come down and start breakfast for everyone." He swung his legs over the edge of the bed and rose, walking into the bathroom.

The kids were still asleep, and I turned the furnace up so our house would be toasty warm when they awoke. The beauty of working only a couple minutes from our house was that I didn't need to wake up early. When I used to commute into Seattle every day, I would spend at least an hour driving into work from Ericksville and the same going home. It had been pretty miserable. Adam had continued to do the commute after we had kids, but now that he was working out of an office in downtown Ericksville, he had the same enviable commute as I did.

I yawned. Even with the short commute, I still hated mornings. Half-asleep, I plodded downstairs and turned on the coffee pot. Without coffee, there was no chance I'd be able to handle whatever the day could throw at me.

3

*A*lthough we did sometimes help clients by picking up items for their events, the Boathouse didn't officially have a vehicle for this purpose. Luckily, my father-in-law, Lincoln, owned a truck and I'd convinced him to let me borrow it to retrieve the decorations from Angela's house. His pickup truck had a long bed plus a crew cab, and it was absolutely gigantic in comparison to my minivan. The blue paint on it still shone as bright as the day he'd bought it brand-new twenty years prior.

"Now, please be careful with her." He dangled the keys in front of him.

I reached for the set of keys, but he didn't let go easily.

"Sorry," he said, with a foolish grin. "I know you'll take good care of the truck."

"I will."

He relinquished the keys. I hopped into the driver's seat and closed the door. I hadn't wanted to tell my father-in-law that this was the biggest vehicle I'd ever driven and to tell the truth—I was a little scared.

He was still in his driveway, waiting for me to leave, so I

gave him a brave wave and started up the truck. I inched it out of the driveway, gaining a little speed after I turned onto the main road. In my rearview mirror, I could see Lincoln still standing there with his hands in his pockets. *No pressure, Jill.* I had a feeling he wouldn't be too happy if I did something to his truck.

On the way over, rain started to fall from the sky in fat droplets that blurred the windshield. I flicked on the windshield wipers but the visibility wasn't great. Twenty minutes later, as I neared Angela's house, the rain stopped.

I arrived at the house safely, which I recognized from the plethora of Halloween pictures I'd rifled through. Her house was in an older part of town, in the area between Ericksville and Everton, right on the bluff overlooking Puget Sound. Houses like this didn't come cheaply and it looked like hers had a double lot. The extra space allowed them to have a carport in the front, and a white car was parked in the driveway. I managed to maneuver the big truck into the driveway behind it.

When I got out of the truck, my legs were shaky and I stood for a moment to settle my nerves, basking in the October sun that had appeared after the rain clouds passed through the area. The air held the distinctive smell of recent rain and the grass and flowers in front of the house sparkled as the sun hit the drops of moisture that remained on the plants.

I wasn't looking forward to moving the decorations, but at least it wasn't raining now. I was a little worried that there didn't appear to be more people here to help. I knocked on Angela's front door, but instead of her, a man came to the door.

"Hi," I said. "I'm here to get the Halloween decorations for the haunted house."

Recognition dawned on his face. "Oh, yeah. Sure. Let me get Angela."

He disappeared into the house, limping as he walked. He shouted out her name, but returned a few minutes later wearing a puzzled expression.

"I don't know where my wife went. I've been in my study all day and haven't ventured outside." He pointed at the white car I'd parked next to. "Her car's out front, so she should be around. Maybe she walked down to the corner market or something."

My jaw clenched and I forced myself to relax. I found myself doing that a lot of that when it came to Angela. She'd asked me to come and pick up the decorations and she couldn't even be bothered to show up? And where were the other helpers? She'd promised me she'd enlist some help.

"I can show you where she keeps everything though. I'm sure she'll be back soon." He turned away from me to slip on some sneakers from an alcove just inside the front door. They were splattered with specks of wet mud, reminding me to clean off my own shoes before I got back into the truck. Lincoln wouldn't appreciate me tracking dirt into his pristine truck.

The man led me down the steps of the front porch and through an imposing wrought iron gate with a sticky latch, leading to the back of their house, where a large shed had been erected. A woman stood near the shed, fiddling with the lock.

"Can I help you?" Angela's husband asked.

She turned, and I recognized Lisa, the group leader from the MUMs meeting.

Her face flamed when she saw us. "I was trying to get this stupid padlock back on the door. I found it on the ground when I got here, but I can't seem to get it to stay on the door."

"Don't worry about it," he said. "When you're done, I'll lock up again." He looked around. "Did my wife let you in?"

"No, I haven't seen her, but she told me the shed was around back. She was supposed to meet me here." Lisa opened the shed doors partway.

"Me too." I peeked into the shed, which held several shelves piled high with Halloween paraphernalia. A musty smell assailed my nose and light streaming through a single window in the shed revealed dust floating in the air. However, the boxes of decorations looked to be in good condition. A large sarcophagus had a place of honor against the back wall. "Whoa. This is way more than I expected." I was going to need to make several trips between here and the Boathouse, which would really cut into my day.

"Hey," called out a familiar voice.

I turned to see Desi come around the side of the house and I walked toward her to help her with the latch on the gate.

"Hey. What are you doing here?" In my phone call with Angela that morning, she'd said she'd try to round up a few volunteers, but I hadn't expected to see my sister-in-law.

"Don't sound so excited to see me," Desi said. "I can go back home if you'd like."

"No, no. Please don't."

She laughed. "I called Angela today to touch base with her on the treasurer position and somehow found myself roped into helping today. I think she may have called Lisa too to see if anyone in the MUMs group was available to help out today."

"That's what happens when you volunteer for a single

23

job with an organization—you find yourself doing so much more," I said smugly. "I told you that you'd regret it."

She shrugged. "You seem to have ended up here too."

I rolled my eyes at her. "It's my job."

"Yeah, well, I wouldn't have said I'd do it, except she was going on and on about her assistant Mindy going through a bitter divorce and how much it was affecting the quality of her work because she should have had time to help out today. Angela was so mad and I though her rant would never end. I finally said I'd help move the decorations so that she'd let me off the phone."

"Ah. That does sound like Angela." I laughed. "And I am glad you're here." I smiled at her.

"Anyway, I heard you all talking back here when I pulled up. This place is amazing! I didn't even know there were still houses like this in Ericksville. My mom would love to see it. Maybe Angela would consider adding it to the Ericksville Historical Society's house tour." She gestured to the shed. "Is that where all the magic is kept?"

I nodded. "Take a look."

She walked over to the shed and greeted Lisa and introduced herself to Angela's husband before ducking her head into the shed, pulling on a string to turn on the overhead light. "Whoa." When she turned to face us, her eyes were wide.

Angela's husband laughed. "My wife takes Halloween very seriously." His voice took on a concerned note. "Which is why I'm surprised she's not here to meet all of you. She usually wants to make sure care is taken with all of her decorations. Some of them took weeks to create."

"Do you want us to wait until she gets back?" I asked, shifting my weight between my feet. I crossed my fingers behind my back, hoping he'd say no.

"Uh." He glanced at the shed. "I guess it's ok. She did mention you'd all be coming to move everything over to the event space. I'm sorry I can't help more, but my asthma has been flaring up lately and I'm trying to avoid strenuous activities. Plus, everything in there has a year's worth of dust on it."

"No worries." Lisa set the lock down on the concrete pad next to the shed and pushed the door all the way open. "Now, what should we grab first?"

"How about the smaller decorations in the front. I'd like to load the sarcophagus into the truck first, if the three of us can manage it, but we need to move some stuff out of the way to get to it." I assessed the situation, my gaze stopping on some mouse droppings in the corner of the shed. I forced myself to not think about the possibility that a mouse could jump out at me at any moment.

"We can set the other stuff down on the concrete," Desi said, pointing to where Lisa had placed the lock. "I think I see a tarp in there that we can put down to keep everything dry."

I pictured Angela's reaction if we let any of her decorations get wet or muddy and shuddered.

"Good plan, Desi!" Lisa beamed at her and grabbed a few things off the shelving unit.

I marveled at Lisa's energy and seemingly constant state of chipperness. I didn't know her very well yet, but I suspected she must consume a lot of coffee or energy drinks every day.

We moved everything smaller away, then loaded a few medium-sized items into the truck bed.

I eyed the sarcophagus. "I think we can get it out of there now."

"Let's try!" Lisa sprinted over to it and grabbed the top. It barely moved. She laughed. "I think I'm going to need some help. It feels like there's a real mummy inside."

I squeezed into the gap between the shelves, all the while trying not to think of the possibility that rodents might live in the shed, and wrapped my fingers around the back of the container. With both of us moving it, the sarcophagus inched along the ground until we had it outside of the shed.

"Whew!" Lisa wiped away sweat from her brow with a tissue. "That wasn't easy!"

"Are we going to be able to move that all the way to the truck?" Desi regarded the sarcophagus with doubt. "I wish we had a dolly."

"We're going to try." We were going to get all of this stuff moved to the Boathouse today because I didn't want to have to borrow Lincoln's truck again. If we'd had another person, it would have been better. Where was Angela anyway? This was her project. "I think if one of us holds onto the middle and one of us carries each end, we should be able to lift it. Watch the mud, ladies. We don't want to slip." I checked the sky. The air held the acrid scent of recent rain, but the clouds drifting across the sunny sky weren't as dark as the rainclouds that had hovered over us earlier.

"No kidding." Desi lifted a mud-covered foot off the ground. "We could have done without that rainstorm drenching everything."

"We can do this! On the count of three, let's lift. One, two, three!" Lisa shouted.

We tilted the coffin backward and she lifted the bottom of it in the air.

"This isn't so bad," I said as the three of us moved it toward the front yard. It was heavy, but it looked like we'd make it.

"Nope, not too bad," Desi said, carefully picking her way backward along the grass. Suddenly, she pitched to the side and slid, unable to get her footing on the muddy grass. Without Desi anchoring the end of the sarcophagus, we were powerless to stop it from falling. Lisa and I jumped away from it instinctively so our feet wouldn't get squished. We watched in horror as it crashed to the ground, hitting the grass with an unsettling thud.

Desi stood, brushing mud off of her jeans. "I'm so sorry, guys. I tripped on a rock or something."

I glanced at the ground near where she'd been walking. Someone had left a paver half buried in the grass. I pointed to it. "Looks like that's the culprit."

"That's a dumb spot to leave a piece of concrete," Desi grumbled.

"No kidding!" said Lisa. "Do you think this thing is broken?" She stared down at the end of the sarcophagus by her feet.

My heart stopped. Angela would kill us if anything happened to her precious decorations, and this one looked particularly real. I circled it, searching for any signs of damage.

When I finished, I took a deep breath. "I think it's ok. Let's get it into the truck before anything else happens to it."

We each picked it up in the same places we'd been assigned to before, but something felt different.

"Stop. I think the lid is loose." I hadn't seen the lid separating from the base when it was on the ground, but it was apparent from this angle. We gently lowered it to the ground and I pushed on the lid to reseat it, Desi reaching over to help me.

"It's not working. Maybe we need to take it off

27

completely and then place it back on the base." Desi ran her finger around the open seal.

I shrugged. Her suggestion just might work.

We shimmied the lid off and pushed it to one side of the container.

Lisa was the first to look inside. "Oh my goodness!" Her skin paled and she stumbled over to the bushes and vomited.

Desi and I looked at each other, then peered into the coffin at the same time.

A woman's body had been stuffed into the sarcophagus. Cold, blue, unblinking eyes stared straight up at us. Strangulation marks ringed her neck.

Desi sucked in her breath and pointed. "I've never met her, but is that Angela Laveaux?"

4

——————

I distanced myself from the grimace on the woman's face and took a better look at her features. She had round cheeks, a pert nose, and minimal makeup. She wore jeans and a T-shirt, both of which appeared to be dry. "No, it's not Angela. I don't think I've ever seen her before."

Lisa was dabbing at her mouth with a tissue. "That's Mindy Danvers."

"Who?" I moved my attention from the woman's body to Lisa.

"Mindy is, uh ... was, Angela's secretary at the district offices of MUMs." Lisa's face turned green again and she ran over to the other side of the yard.

"I thought that coffin was too heavy to be fake." Desi stared at the body. "But how did she get in there? And where's Angela?"

All I could do was shake my head. How was this happening again? There had to be a limit to how many dead bodies one person could discover in their lifetime—and I must already be at my quota.

And where was Angela? She'd promised to meet us here, but instead she was missing and her assistant had turned up dead.

A chill ran through my veins. Had Angela been killed too? Or kidnapped? I didn't like her much, but I didn't want her dead either.

"I guess it's time to call the police," Desi said in a dull voice.

"Yeah." I really didn't want to have to do that. I was beginning to have a not-so-great reputation with the police department in this town.

"Can you do it?" I pleaded. "You're a policeman's wife. It won't be so bad coming from you."

"Are you kidding me? If they find out it's me calling, Tomàs will hear all about this and he'll be upset and worried about me being involved with another death."

"Fine, I'll call." I patted the front pocket of my zip-front sweatshirt, but there weren't any hard bumps in it. "I think I forgot my cell phone in the truck."

"Go. I'll stay here with the body," Desi said.

Lisa had disappeared, probably to avoid vomiting again. I went out to my truck and retrieved the cell phone from my purse. As I closed the door, I heard a noise behind me.

"It doesn't look like you've done much here," Angela said. "I thought you'd be almost done by now. I had to go to the store to pick up a few things and the stupid cashier messed everything up. It took forever." She held up a plastic bag containing what looked like the outlines of a tabloid magazine, a bag of chips, and a bottle of soda.

I looked at her in disbelief. Had she been late on purpose so she wouldn't have to help move the decorations?

"Where is everyone, anyway? Lisa and Desi were supposed to be here already." She scanned the yard.

I sighed. "Come into the backyard."

She followed me around the side of the house, stopping short when she saw the lid to the sarcophagus lying on the ground.

"What have you done? How could you be so careless? That's an antique. I can't replace it. Oh, I hope it's not broken."

Before I had a chance to explain, she ran over to the object. "Oh my." She covered her mouth with her hand. "Is that Mindy?"

"I think so." I checked her expression as I spoke.

She blinked her eyes. "What happened to her? Why was she even here? I asked her to help today, but she said she didn't have time."

"I don't know," I said truthfully. "When we were carrying it out, Desi tripped on a piece of concrete over there and we accidentally dropped it. I noticed the lid was ajar and realized we needed to take it off first to reposition it in the grooves. That's when we found her like that."

She couldn't seem to take her eyes off the body. "Poor Mindy."

"Angela, you're back." Her husband came into the backyard. "What's going on out here?"

Angela pointed at the open coffin and he walked toward it.

His eyes widened when he saw what was in it and he backed away. "No. Uh, uh. There's not a body in my backyard." He continued retreating until he reached the house, then disappeared inside of it.

I looked at Angela, raising my eyebrows.

She shrugged. "Drew doesn't deal well with stress."

She seemed calmer now about finding her employee's body in her backyard.

I held up the phone I held in my hand. "I'm calling the police now."

She nodded and stalked over to the shed. "You've done hardly anything."

Desi's eyes narrowed and her mouth formed a wide O. She muttered something under her breath that I couldn't quite hear, but I was pretty sure wasn't complimentary. She walked over to me, standing close.

"I see what you mean about Angela now. Is she even upset about this? Or does she only care about her decorations and the haunted house?"

"I don't know." My eyes followed Angela. "She certainly isn't acting like a normal person who's discovered their employee dead in their backyard."

"No kidding."

I called the police and they promised to send emergency personnel to the scene.

"Thank you for not mentioning me," Desi said. "Tomàs was pretty upset about what happened last time we discovered a body. I thought there was no way he was going to let us stay at Thunder Lake Resort after that."

"Me too." I was quiet, thinking about the other bodies we'd found and the situations we'd found ourselves in, like the time we'd almost been drowned in Lake Elinor. "This time we don't know the victim and we don't have a horse in this race. There shouldn't be any reason for us to get involved."

"Agreed. I'd e-mailed Angela about treasurer stuff, but I never met her in person until just now. I'm staying out of this one." She and I walked over to the house's back porch to wait for the police to arrive.

The police showed up five minutes later and immediately took control of the scene. Desi and I were standing closest to Mindy's body, so they interviewed us first.

"And you just happened to drop the coffin thing and the lid dropped open to reveal the body?" The policewoman scrutinized Desi and I.

Lisa had disappeared completely and Desi gave the police what little contact information we had for her.

I nodded vigorously. "Yes. Well, kind of. We dropped it and then the lid loosened, so we had to take it off to reposition it. That's when we saw her like that." I averted my eyes from Mindy's body. The crime scene technicians were busy photographing everything and taking samples of what appeared to be every surface in the area.

"I tripped over that piece of concrete and the whole sarcophagus came down." Desi pointed helpfully at the paver, then glared at it.

"Uh huh." She jotted something down on her notepad. "And where was Ms. Laveaux while all this was happening?"

"She was at the store." Desi said, pointing at the discarded shopping bag on the porch.

"Well, she told us she was at the store." My eyes darted to Angela, who was standing next to her husband, comforting him, but looking unperturbed herself.

The officer's gaze shot up sharply. "What do you mean, 'she told you'? Do you think she was somewhere else?"

I shrugged. "I don't know. She was supposed to meet us here to help us load the truck. All of this needed to get to the Boathouse downtown today. When I arrived, she wasn't here and her husband had no clue where she was."

"Do you know if Ms. Laveaux had any grudge against Ms. Danvers?" Her eyes drilled into my face, making me squirm under the scrutiny.

How was I supposed to know if there was bad blood

between them? I'd never met Mindy Danvers while she was alive.

"Not that I know of, but I've never met Mindy before and I wouldn't say I was close to Angela Laveaux, so I'm not the best person to ask."

"Is there someone who would have a better idea?"

Desi piped up. "Lisa Aldane. She's the group leader for our local MUMs group and reports to Angela, who's the local director. I believe they've known each other for a while."

"MUMs group?" she asked.

"More United Mothers," Desi said. "It's a bunch of moms who get together to chat and have our babies play—there are exercise classes as well. Jill and I joined last week, so we don't know too much about it, but Lisa can explain it better."

She scribbled something on her pad and then snapped it shut. "Thank you for your time. I'll be in touch with you if we need anything else." She tilted his head to the side and peered at Desi. "Say, your name sounds familiar. Are you related to Tomàs Torres? He's a policeman here in town."

Desi froze, then sighed. "Yes, he's my husband."

The officer grinned at her. "Ah, I thought so. It's nice meeting you Ms. Torres." She turned to me. "And you too, Ms. Andrews."

"Nice to meet you too," we said in unison.

She jetted off toward Angela and Drew Laveaux, leaving us standing alone.

"Now what?" Desi asked. "I don't think they're going to let us take any of the decorations home with us today."

"I don't think so either." I glanced toward the front yard where my truck was parked. "They've taken everything from the shed out of my truck too, in case it contained any clues. I sure hope they aren't keeping everything for long." The haunted house was scheduled to open in a little over two weeks, and if we didn't get Angela's stuff back in time, I didn't think the decorations I could buy at the local department store were going to cut it. We'd be the laughingstock of all of Ericksville if all our haunted house had was a few paper skeletons and peeled-grape eyeballs.

"It'll be ok." She gave me a quick hug. "And if they don't return the decorations in time, we'll figure it out together."

I wasn't positive she was right, but at this point, I appreciated the reassurance. "Thanks. Should we go home now?" I gestured to all the decorations strewn across the grass. "I feel bad leaving these here."

"There's nothing we can do. Besides, they belong to Angela. She can make arrangements with the police to get everything returned in time for the haunted house. You're responsible for the actual event, not for the decorations. Leave that to her," Desi said firmly.

"Ok." I walked toward the front yard, with Desi following me. "I'll see you for dinner? You and the kids are still coming over, right?"

"Yep. Tomàs has to work, but I've got all the veggies for the taco and burrito bar in my fridge. I'll see you at six."

"See you." I got into the truck and drove it back to Lincoln's house, parking it next to his car in the driveway, before getting back into my own vehicle. My minivan felt tiny in comparison to the big truck, but it was pleasingly familiar. After the day I'd had already, any sense of normalcy was a big plus.

5
---

*D*esi arrived at our house for dinner a little after six. As soon as I opened the door, Anthony brushed past his mom and ran into the house, shouting Mikey's name.

"Sorry I'm late. Lina just woke up from her nap." She held the baby out to me. "Can you take her so I can go back to the car and get the taco fixings? I swear, mothers should have been blessed with eight arms like an octopus."

I smiled at the image. That would have been helpful.

"No problem." I took Lina from her and snuggled her against me.

When she returned with an armload of containers of freshly cut veggies and shredded cheese, I handed Lina off to Adam and we took everything into the kitchen and set it down on the counter. Our kitchen smelled strongly of taco seasoning and ground beef. Goldie was sniffing the air from the living room.

"We'd better eat before Goldie downs it all," Desi said, laughing.

We brought everything over to the dinner table and called for the kids to wash up and come sit down.

Desi knelt down by a bottom cupboard in the kitchen. "Where are the plastic cups for the boys?" She looked up at me with a puzzled expression on her face. "Aren't they usually down here?"

I rolled my eyes. "Adam has been doing some rearranging in his spare time. He felt they'd be better up there." I pointed at an upper cupboard.

She smirked. "Ok ..."

"I know." I laughed. "I keep having to search for things, but at least he's taking an interest in things at home."

The boys bumbled into the dining room, followed by a toddling Ella and Adam carrying Lina. He helped the girls into their high chairs at the table and we all sat down. Mikey and Anthony each placed two taco shells on their plates and piled them high with beef and cheese.

Desi appraised their choices. "I want to see some veggies on there, boys."

"But, Mom! I hate veggies," Anthony whined. Mikey tossed some tomatoes on his plate and his cousin's plate, then smiled at us.

"Lettuce too," I said. He begrudgingly followed my request.

I had just taken a bite of an amazing smelling burrito when my work cell phone rang. I eyed it. Should I answer, or let it go? I didn't want to offend any of our clients by not answering, so I folded the napkin in my lap and stood from the table.

"Jill. It's dinner time," Adam said. "Can't they wait until later?"

My eyes darted to the phone. "I'm just going to check and see who it is."

He sighed.

By the time I got to the phone on my desk, the caller had hung up, but they'd left a voicemail. I peeked at my family, but they'd gone back to eating, so I pressed play to hear the message.

"Hi, Jill. This is Drew Laveaux, Angela's husband." He sighed. "I'm calling because Angela's been arrested for Mindy's murder."

I gasped, causing Adam and Desi to stare at me. I held up a finger and finished listening to the message.

"She didn't do it, of course, but the police think they have evidence against her." He sighed again. "Anyway, she wanted me to call you and let you know that the police said they'll deliver all of the decorations to the Boathouse in a few days. This is so important to Angela—until she's released, I don't want any planning to get behind."

He hung up and I stared at my phone for a moment.

"Jill! Who was that?" Desi asked.

Adam regarded me with concern. "Are you ok? You look pale."

I plopped down in my chair at the table, still a little shell-shocked. "That was Angela's husband. She's been arrested for the ..." I looked over at Mikey and Anthony, who were now looking at me wide-eyed. "... M-U-R-D-E-R of Mindy Danvers."

Desi gasped. "Whoa." She glanced furtively at the boys and said in a lower voice. "Do you think she did it?"

"Wait. Is this the same Angela that's been driving you crazy for months?" Adam asked. "She's involved with this?"

I nodded. I'd told him that Desi and I had discovered another body today, but I hadn't given him many other details.

I looked over at Desi. "I don't know. I guess she could

have done it. She's not the nicest woman in the world, but if I'd been placing bets on who would be killed, it would have been her, not her assistant."

"Killed?" Mikey's eyes were as round as plates.

Oops. I'd let too much slip. "Honey, someone died today, but don't worry, the police will find out what happened, ok?"

"Uncle Tomàs will figure it out?" he asked.

"Uncle Tomàs and his friends at work." I spooned some salsa onto my plate with shaking hands and then changed the subject. "How was school today?"

The boys jumped over themselves telling us about their latest projects in Creative Arts at the preschool.

"And the Harvest Carnival is in only a month," Anthony said solemnly. "I'm going to win a goldfish this year."

"A month?" My eyes met Desi's. Were they having it in November?

She smiled. "I think you mean a week, honey."

"Yeah. A week, that's what I said." He went back to eating his taco, racing his cousin to see who could finish first.

"Are you volunteering at the carnival this year?" Desi asked.

I groaned. "I should probably get in touch with Danielle or Nancy about it." I tried my best to stay away from Nancy Davenport, my archnemesis at Busy Bees Preschool, but Danielle, the school's owner, had very kindly allowed me to register Mikey after I forgot to fill out the paperwork on time, so I owed her. "I'm not running the goldfish booth though." We'd had a bad string of goldfish deaths since the last Harvest Carnival and I didn't want to deal with any more death. At that thought, the memory of Mindy's cold eyes staring out at me flashed through my brain. I pushed the image out, refusing to let it spoil our family dinner.

"Let's ask if we can run the bounce house. The boys will

spend most of their time in there anyway." Desi bit into her taco, the shell crunching beneath her teeth.

"Sounds good." I ate my meal and the boys finished theirs.

"Can we go play?" Mikey held up his plate, which was empty save a few streaks of sour cream. "See, I'm a member of the clean plate club."

I smiled. "Yes, you can both go play. But don't wake up the babies." Ella had finished her dinner and both of the girls had fallen asleep in the living room. Neither of them was very happy when woken up prematurely from a nap.

When the boys were out of earshot, Desi turned to me.

"Do you think Angela killed her?"

"I don't know. I never got a crazy vibe from her the whole time I've been working for her, but you never can tell about people." I felt Adam's eyes on me. I'd been in danger too many times recently and I knew he worried about me. Suddenly, something occurred to me. "No. I don't think she did it. There's no way."

"Why are you so sure?" Desi asked.

"Because Angela wouldn't do anything to jeopardize the haunted house." After uttering it out loud, I realized how true that was. "If she was going to kill someone, it wouldn't be at Halloween."

Desi pressed her lips together, contemplating what I'd said.

"You're probably right. Anyone who put that much effort into Halloween would never want to be locked up in jail instead of out decorating for it." She fiddled with her fork. "But if she didn't do it, who did?"

The three of us stared at each other.

"I don't like you being involved with this." Adam folded

his napkin and leaned back in his chair without taking his eyes off of me.

"I know, but this is my job. I have to manage the haunted house event at the Boathouse. Other than that, I don't really have anything to do with this Mindy person." I smiled at him tentatively. "Believe me, I don't want to be in danger either."

"And the only connection I have with this is being the new treasurer for our MUMs group. So I suppose I would have had more interactions with Mindy eventually, but so far I'd only corresponded with her via e-mail. Neither of us had ever met her in person." Desi stood to clear the plates from the table.

"But you know Angela and it sounds like she's in the middle of this. Did her husband say why the police suspect her of murdering Mindy?" Adam stood too, collecting everyone's water glasses and bringing them into the kitchen.

I shook my head. "No, he didn't say why. Just that he didn't know when she'd get out and she wanted me to continue with the haunted house preparations. Like I said, there's no way she would have done anything that could cause the haunted house to fail. She's obsessed with it."

"Ok," he said finally. "But promise me, if anything happens that makes you feel in danger, get out of that situation."

"Aye, aye." I saluted him and laughed, trying to lighten the mood.

He frowned at me. "Jill, I'm serious."

I sobered. "I know. And I swear I'll be careful." I glanced at Desi. "Both of us will." Beside me, she nodded.

"Ok then. I've got some work to do in my study. Do you need any help with the kids tonight or is it ok for me to sign off now?"

"Nope, I'm fine."

"We'd better get going anyway," Desi said, gathering up her food containers. "Anthony's bedtime is fast approaching and I think I hear Lina waking up. She's going to want to eat soon."

I helped her out to the car with the kids and food, lingering outside by the open sliding side door of her minivan.

"Are we still going to the MUMs meeting tomorrow?" I held my hand on the door, while I watched as Anthony fastened his car seat restraints.

"Yep. It's going to be weird though." Desi grimaced. "Lisa will be there and it was like she just vanished earlier today. I wonder if the police caught up with her to ask her questions too."

"Yeah. It was strange how she disappeared." I thought about when I'd arrived at Angela's house this afternoon. "You know, I didn't mention this before to you, but when I got to Angela's house, her husband was inside and Lisa was standing in front of the unlocked shed door. Drew had no idea she was there."

"What does that mean? That she could have done it?" Desi stopped what she was doing and looked at me.

"Done what, Mommy?" Anthony asked.

"Nothing, sweetie." She tousled his hair, then turned back to me. "We'll talk tomorrow, ok?"

I nodded and she got in her vehicle and drove away. Back in the house, I helped Mikey get ready for bed and gave Ella a bottle and bath before placing her into a warm sleep sack in her crib. I carried out all of the bedtime routines on autopilot. Something wasn't adding up here. Had Mindy arrived before everyone else and been attacked by some random person? Or was it someone else? Angela? Lisa? Drew? Who had unlocked the shed anyway?

I gave up thinking about it and, with the kids taken care of, ran a bubble bath for myself. I lay back in the warm water, trying to wash away the day. Rain pattered onto the skylight above me, providing comforting background noise for relaxation. The water swished under my fingertips as I lazily waved my hands back and forth under the surface.

Once Halloween was over, the mad holiday rush would swoop in and take over my life. Thanksgiving meals, family, Christmas trees, and gifts. A rush of guilt came over me. Here I was worrying about holiday stress and a woman had died today.

The water had chilled and I rose from it, drying off with a fluffy towel. I got into bed and turned on some easy listening music to fall asleep to, hoping that sleep would come just as easily. Instead, thoughts of Mindy swirled through my brain, making sleep hard to achieve. Sometime during the night, exhaustion took over my body, but my dreams were full of terrifying mummies coming alive to terrorize the town.

6
_____

$\mathcal{T}$he next day, Desi and I stood outside the library with our hands in our pockets and our babies in their strollers in front of us. It was only two o'clock, but the temperature had dropped since morning and now we and our babies were bundled up, ready to go on our first stroller walk with the MUMs group.

"Hello, girls!" Lisa said as she arrived, pushing her son in a stroller that probably cost as much as my first car. "Lovely day, isn't it?" She wore brand-name yoga pants and a form-fitting jacket, with colorful sneakers rounding out her ensemble.

"It is." Desi looked around. "Where is everyone else?"

"Oh. Everyone's always late." Lisa frowned. "I swear, I'm the only one in this organization that can tell time."

I cocked my head to the side. Our ever-peppy friend had a touch of negativity. I wasn't sure whether that made me like her or dislike her more. At least it made her more human.

Lisa's son stirred in his seat and she fussed over his crocheted Spiderman hat.

44

A few more moms arrived and, at a quarter after the hour, Lisa led us out onto the sidewalk at a brisk pace. "We're going to head over to the park today," she said. "The trees there will be beautiful."

She was right. I'd thought the MUMs outing would be one more stressor in my life, but I had to admit, I was enjoying the walk with the other moms. High above us, gold and orange leaves clung persistently to the tree branches, occasionally letting go and floating down to the ground. The general mood at the park was upbeat, with people taking their dogs out for a run or their children to the playground.

Desi sidled up to me, jarring me back to reality. "Did Lisa say anything to you about yesterday?"

In all of my musings about peace, I'd completely forgotten how odd Lisa had acted the day before.

"No. I didn't mention it either. The police must have talked to her, right?"

"I'd assume so. I could probably ask Tomàs, although he won't be able to tell me much about an active investigation."

"Plus, then he'd know you were involved with it."

"Good point. Ok, that's out. With any luck, that police officer I met yesterday won't have said anything to him." She narrowed her eyes at Lisa as she pranced along the sidewalk about twenty feet in front of us. "You said she was the first person there, right?"

"Well, yeah, except Mindy must have beaten her there and whoever killed her, of course."

"Hmm." She wiped at her dripping nose with a Kleenex. "And Angela was nowhere to be seen. So either of them could have killed Mindy. But why?"

"I have no clue. But the only thing connecting them to each other was MUMs, right?"

We both eyed the other moms with suspicion. If Lisa or

45

Angela had killed Mindy for a reason having to do with MUMs, any of these women could be a suspect as well. Suddenly, things in the group didn't seem so peaceful.

"We're being ridiculous, right?" Desi asked. "Mindy's death probably had nothing to do with MUMs."

"Probably." I stopped to tie my shoe, causing Desi and me to fall further behind the rest of the group. "We could leave them all right now," I whispered.

She put her hands on her hips. "Jill! We can't do that. Plus, I'm the treasurer now. I can't just ditch them."

"Ok, ok. It was just a fleeting thought."

"Yeah, well, send it away." She wrapped her hands around her stroller's handle. "But in all honesty, it wouldn't hurt to be careful."

I stood and brushed dirt off of my knee where I'd knelt on the ground. "Let's just try to have fun today."

"Agreed." She smiled at me and we hurried to catch up with the rest of the group, which had stopped in a circle in front of us like a miniature wagon train.

We joined the circle and performed leg lifts and squats while holding on to our strollers. It was a surprisingly effective workout, but not very exciting, leaving me plenty of time to look at all of the babies in the group. My eyes flitted between the strollers. What was with the crocheted hats? I'd thought the Spiderman hat Lisa's son was sporting was cute, but each baby had an ornately crocheted hat. Ella and Lina's knit caps were plain in comparison.

"All right. Everyone on the ground for five push-ups. And I want to see all of you ladies try," Lisa shouted.

I nudged Desi as we lowered ourselves to the ground to do push-ups.

"Do you see all of their hats?" I whispered, supporting my weight with my knees. Carrying two little kids around all the time had given me some upper body strength, but I'd never been able to do a proper push-up.

"No, why?" she asked through gritted teeth. Her arms trembled as she completed her fifth push-up. She stood and surveyed all of the babies. "Oh. I see what you mean." She shrugged. "Maybe it's the newest craze and we're late to the party."

I jumped up from the ground and shook my arms out. Lisa had broken the circle and we now followed her as she jogged down a trail. "Maybe. Sheesh. I'm out of shape."

"Yeah, me too," she said, huffing and puffing as we came out at the parking lot and Lisa announced that the class was over. "Maybe I should add some salads to the BeansTalk's menu."

"Did you say the BeansTalk?" a woman in black just ahead of us said, not in the least bit out of breath. She swiveled her stroller around to face us. Her daughter sported a crocheted Minnie Mouse hat with ear warmers.

Desi nodded. "I did. I'm the owner."

"Oh, I love that place!" she exclaimed. "It's so cute with the little play area in the back. My toddler loves it."

"Thanks," Desi said warmly. "I try to make it a welcoming place for parents. I know how difficult it can be to find places to take the little ones when it's raining."

"Definitely. I'm already getting sick of staring at the walls of our house." She glanced at our babies. "Do you have any other children? My mother is watching my older one."

"We both do," I said. "Four-year-old boys. They're at preschool now."

"Oh." She sniffed. "I'm not planning on putting my children into school until they're in kindergarten. I feel like when you have young kids, you should be the one raising them, not having strangers do so."

"Oh, really," Desi said politely. "Our boys love their preschool."

"I'm sure they do," the woman said. "It's probably a great option if you have to work."

"Uh huh." I turned to Desi. "Speaking of which, I need to get back to work."

She nodded. "It was nice meeting you."

"You too," the woman said, wheeling her daughter around.

Desi and I walked back to the BeansTalk with the babies.

"That's what I mean about the stay-at-home moms. They're always so smug," I said as I struggled to push Ella's stroller over a tree root.

Desi shrugged. "Everyone's entitled to their own opinion."

"I guess." I was quiet for a moment. I'd been the stay-at-home mom for a few years and had only recently gone back into the workforce. "I may be a little sensitive about it because I worry about Adam's practice not taking off the way we thought it would."

She stopped at a crosswalk. "Is everything ok? Adam hasn't said anything to me about things not going well at work."

I sighed. "Yeah, I think it will be fine. It takes a while to build up a client base. It's just that I've turned over most of the bills to Adam and it makes me a little paranoid when I don't have control over all of our finances. Plus, I do worry about Mikey being at preschool for so long every day."

She laughed and pushed the stroller across the street. "Those boys love it there. I can barely drag Anthony away from his friends when I come to pick him up. You're worrying about nothing."

"I know. Mikey is like that too." Was I letting that other mom get to me? I hated second-guessing myself and the choices we'd made for our kids. I knew Mikey loved his school and was probably much happier there than being bored at home with me, but still, there was that niggling doubt.

"Well, this is me," Desi said in front of the café. "I'll call you later, ok?"

"Talk to you later." I continued on with Ella to the Boathouse, where Beth would watch her while I finished up some important work. I had a proposal to write up for a company party and several suppliers to call before the end of the day. Life was full of choices and, for now, working at the Boathouse was where I needed to be, but that didn't mean I wasn't raising my kids.

7

*A*ngela was a brilliant artist and creative, but she was a hard act to follow and these photos of previous haunted houses were all I had to work with. *Great.* I threw them down and they cascaded out across the surface of my desk. I leaned forward, resting my head on my hands.

With Angela out of commission, I was on my own for planning the haunted house. I hoped they'd release her soon, but the court system was refusing to allow her out on bail. She'd played her design ideas close to her chest and now it was coming back to bite us both. I was fairly certain that she wouldn't be happy if we copied things that had been done before. Someone knocked lightly on my half-closed door. I looked up and sighed.

"That bad?" Desi asked, raising her eyebrows. A faint aroma of something sweet drifted through the air. I hoped she'd brought me something from the café and that she wasn't playing an evil trick on me by wearing a new sugar-scented perfume.

I grimaced. "Yes. Angela hadn't given me her designs yet, if she even planned to do so. She's rather secretive about things. Now, I find myself planning a haunted house on my own."

"Ooh." Desi motioned to the pictures. "Can't you copy what she did before?"

I nodded. "I can, but I'm sure when she's released she'll just change everything I've already done. I'm not sure it makes sense to start decorating before she's out."

"But what if they don't let her out anytime soon?" Desi reached into her bag and removed a paper sack bearing the name of her café.

My mouth watered. Breakfast had been too long ago. "They have to, right? I mean, what evidence do they have to hold her?"

Desi shrugged. "According to what the police released to the press, she'd made threats to Mindy and was constantly berating her."

"That doesn't seem like enough to hold her. While maybe it should be, it's not a crime to be mean." I gathered up the photos and returned them to a neat stack in the corner of my desk.

"No, but Mindy was found dead at Angela's house. That's pretty damning on its own." She moved slightly and the bag she was holding crackled.

"I guess." I focused in on her. "So what's up? I'm guessing this isn't a social visit."

"Well ..." Desi said.

"Oh no." This was eerily similar to how our conversation had gone before she roped me into joining the MUMs group with her. "What is it now? An all-women's gym class? A Save the Peacocks rally?"

She put her hands on her hips and made a face at me. "No. I don't even like peacocks. They're always strutting around like they own everything." She came over to my desk and sat down opposite me, placing the sack on the desk in front of me. "I was hoping you would come with me to Mindy's funeral."

"Uh." I leaned back in my chair, not removing my eyes from the bag. I was starving, but I wasn't sure if taking the pastry offering meant I'd accepted her request. "I never even met the woman—well, not while she was alive." The image of a very dead woman flashed into my mind.

"Please? I feel like I should go. I never met her in person either, but I corresponded with her a couple of times about treasurer stuff. It seems disrespectful not to go."

"So why do you need me to go with you?"

Desi squirmed in her seat. "I don't know many of the other people there and funerals always make me feel weird. It would be nice to have someone to go with."

I stared at her and grabbed for the bag. It crackled as I opened it and looked inside. An iced brownie with most of its frosting still intact smiled up at me. My mouth salivated and I closed the bag and placed it securely in my desk drawer. Chocolate was always a winner with me, and Desi knew it.

"When is it?"

She glanced down at my desk and then peeked up at me. "Today at three o'clock."

"Today?" I looked at my computer, a sinking feeling rushing through me. I still had a lot to do and I needed to pick Ella up by two because our babysitter had a doctor's appointment that afternoon. "I can't. I have to get Ella and then pick up Mikey too a little later."

She beamed at me. "I already asked Mom. She said she'd pick them both up. Any other objections?"

She had me. I supposed I could finish any work I had leftover that evening.

"Fine. I'll go. But you really owe me after this. I'm supposed to bring four dozen chocolate chip cookies to the Busy Bees Fall Festival. If I go with you, you're making them."

A smile broke out on her face. "Deal. And I won't even tell Nancy that you didn't bake them yourself. You can let her think you slaved over a hot oven for them." She stood. "Thanks, Jill! I'll see you at two p.m., ok?"

I shook my head and grinned. Why did I always let Desi convince me to do these things with her? Ok, she was my sister-in-law and my best friend, but still. Then again, I'd dragged her into plenty of situations of my own and she'd always followed loyally. Plus, she was going to do my baking for the Fall Festival. That was a big item to check off of my list.

"Yes. I'll see you then." I shooed her to the door with the back of my hand. "Now go, I've got a lot of work to do before then."

"Yes, ma'am," she said, saluting me. "Thanks, Jill!" She hurried out the door, leaving me to stare forlornly at the photos once more.

If only I could convince someone to take care of this for me. I was getting to be a pro at helping brides decide on wedding decor, but I was out of my element when it came to tombstones and werewolves. My idea of Halloween decor was to stick a carved pumpkin on our front porch and hope no neighborhood kids smashed it against my door. I gobbled up the brownie and slugged down some cold coffee. Hopefully the sugar and caffeine would inspire creativity.

I got up to get some air, walking down the hallway past Beth's office. She was on the phone, so I continued on, out to the deck overlooking Puget Sound. We'd brought our floating docks in already in preparation for winter and the deck looked small without them attached. A speed boat zipped across the water, churning up the waves behind it and cutting through the peaceful day with its obnoxiously loud motor. Just as soon as it had come by though, it was gone and the waters were calm again.

The sun was shining, but it provided little warmth. A brisk breeze came off the water, making me wish I'd thrown my coat on before I'd come out. I crossed the wooden planks to the railing and leaned against it, breathing deeply of the salt air. The cool temperatures made my nose drip, but they also brought some clarity. I grabbed a Kleenex from my sweater pocket and dabbed at my nose.

I'd figure this out—I always did. Just last month, I had solved a murder and a jewel heist on the same day I managed the Labor Day celebration for my friend Leah's resort. The haunted house might not be as fabulous as something that Angela came up with, but using the photos of her previous haunted house designs, I should be able to cobble something together that would entertain the crowd. And if all else failed, there was always grape eyeballs and spaghetti brains for kids to reach into, right?

8

By afternoon, the weather had turned even colder and I shivered despite the parka I wore over the black dress that I'd come to associate with funerals. Leaves crunched under the heels of my low black pumps and a breeze ruffled the trees and the thin material of my dress.

"How did I let you talk me into this?" I grumbled to Desi as we walked across the parking lot to the church together.

"Four dozen chocolate cookies, remember?" She raised her eyebrows at me.

"Yeah, yeah." I needed to keep reminding myself to keep my eye on the prize. While I enjoyed cooking, I wasn't much on baking, preferring to leave that to my mother-in-law and sister-in-law, who were amazing bakers.

A group of mourners clad in dark colors made their way into the church. Inside, they milled around, viewing a collection of photographs of Mindy. Judging by the images of her, she had been a very serious woman, but the number of people gathered for her funeral indicated that she'd had many friends. I noticed a few photos of her with a teenage girl and I realized I knew very little about her.

Did she have a family? I suddenly felt horrible for the callous attitude I'd had about going to her funeral. She was involved in MUMs, so it seemed likely that she did have children. She was probably someone's mother, someone's wife. She deserved my respect, even if I hadn't known her in life. I walked closer to a photo of Mindy set up on an easel.

Desi touched my arm and peered into my face. "Are you ok?"

"Yeah." My voice cracked.

She gave me a quizzical look, but didn't comment. "Let's get inside. I think the pews are starting to fill up."

I nodded and followed her into the church's sanctuary. We slid to the far side of a pew in the back of the room, which allowed me to see the rest of the mourners. A closed casket was centered in front of the stage, with a bouquet of red and white roses perched on the top. Other flower arrangements were scattered throughout the room, perfuming the air with a sickly-sweet smell.

A minister approached the podium to the left of the casket. With a somber expression on his face, he addressed the mourners. The microphone crackled as he spoke.

"Thank you all for coming today as we say farewell to one of our flock, Mindy Danvers." He cast a glance at the casket. "She was a devoted member of the church and I know everyone will miss her dearly."

A few people in the pews nodded, murmuring among themselves. A dark-haired man in the pew across the aisle from us and two rows up stared at the casket, not speaking to those on either side of him.

I grabbed Desi's arm and whispered, "Isn't that Drew, Angela's husband?"

She squinted at the man and nodded. "I think so but I can't tell for sure. If it is him, what is he doing here?"

"I don't know. Angela did say that Mindy came over to their house sometimes, so maybe they were friends. At the very least, he knew her through Angela." I leaned forward to get a better look at the man, but there were too many people in the way for me to tell for sure if it was Drew.

"Oh, right. That makes sense. Still kind of weird though since his wife is accused of murdering her." She smoothed out her skirt and focused her attention on the man who was currently speaking about how wonderful Mindy had been.

Several people gave eulogies, then a woman in her twenties came up to the podium—the woman I'd seen in the photographs of her as a teenager with Mindy.

She smiled meekly at the audience, her eyes shimmering with tears.

"Thank you for coming. For those of you who don't know me, I'm Stacey Stevens, Mindy's daughter. My mother would have loved to see all of her friends and family here." She smiled again as she turned her head to view everyone in the crowd, but the smile faltered as her gaze landed on a man near the front of the church.

I nudged Desi. "What is that all about?"

"I don't know," she hissed. "I barely knew Mindy, much less her daughter."

A woman who wore her hair up in a tight bun in front of us turned and glared. We quieted and sat up straighter. Soon, the funeral proceedings were over and we trudged out of the sanctuary into a reception room containing tables laden with coffee and butter cookies.

"Should we pay our respects to her daughter?" I was never sure what the etiquette was for attending the funeral of someone you barely knew.

Desi took a deep breath. "I probably should." She pulled on my arm and we approached Mindy's daughter.

"I'm so sorry for your loss," Desi said.

The woman pressed her lips together, as if trying not to cry. "Thank you." She looked from Desi to me. "How did you know my mother?"

"We recently joined a local MUMs group and I volunteered to be the treasurer." Desi looked like she was fighting for something to say about Mindy. "Your mother was very conscientious about her job."

"Thank you. She would have appreciated you saying so." She smiled at us and stuck out her hand. "I'm Stacey Stevens."

"Nice to meet you," Desi said. "Desi Torres."

I held out my hand as well. "I'm Jill Andrews. I didn't know your mother well, but I'm sure she's the reason for how smoothly our MUMs group runs."

Stacey nodded. Another mourner approached her and she turned to talk with them. We made our way to the refreshments table, each grabbing a cup of coffee. We stood there, sipping our coffee for a few minutes, viewing the crowd.

"I hope there are this many people at my funeral," Desi said.

"Me too. She must have been well-liked." I caught sight of Drew Laveaux. "That is Drew. I'm going to go say hi to him. I hope he has some good news about when Angela will be released."

"I'll come too." Desi and I made our way through the crowd toward Drew, who was now close to the exterior door. My feet padded softly on the patterned carpet as I hurried as fast as I could in my dress shoes.

"Drew," I called out softly, not wanting to shout in front of all of the people behind me. He didn't turn around and we followed him out to the parking lot.

"Drew," I said again. This time, he stopped.

He cocked his head to the side.

"Jill—from the Boathouse. I'm working with Angela on the haunted house." I zipped up my coat to keep out the cold.

Recognition dawned on his face. "Ah. Of course." He focused on Desi. "You were there that day too." His expression darkened.

She nodded. "I was."

"I was hoping you might know if Angela will be released soon," I said.

He shook his head. "No. They haven't given me a release date. Her lawyer says it might not be until the arraignment in a few days."

"That's awful," Desi said. "I can't believe they think she did it."

"Me neither." He stuck his hands in his pockets and stared up at the leafless branches of a maple tree. "I figured I should pay my respects to Mindy though. I know Angela would want that."

"Did you know her well? Were she and Angela close?" Desi asked.

"No, not well, but she was over at our house every so often." He frowned. "Angela sometimes needed her help on the weekends." He quickly added. "But they were good friends."

Right. Friends. Of course she needed Mindy's help on the weekend. Off hours didn't seem to matter much to Angela. I didn't say that out loud though. Instead, I just nodded.

"I'm sure Angela will miss her friend." Maybe it was true. Maybe she and Mindy had actually been friends, but I had my doubts. I couldn't picture what it would be like to be friends with Angela Laveaux.

"She will." He was quiet, staring off into the empty branches again. "Well, I'd better get home." He pulled his keys out of his pocket, jingling them against each other.

"Of course," I murmured. Wait, this was my chance to ask him if Angela had written her haunted house plans down anywhere. "I'm sorry to ask, but do you know if Angela had the designs for this year's haunted house somewhere? Without her guidance, I'm a little lost."

He thought about it. "I haven't seen any, but I haven't been in her studio at our house lately either. You're welcome to come by the house to look for them."

A sense of relief came over me. "Thank you so much. I really appreciate it. I know how much this means to Angela and I want to make sure we continue making progress on the decor while she's away."

"Uh huh. Stop by when you have a chance. I work from home, so I'm there most of the time. You know where we live."

"Thank you."

More of the mourners were coming out of the church now and he walked away briskly toward the car I'd seen parked in his driveway. With his wife suspected of Mindy's murder, he probably didn't want to get into too many conversations with her friends and family.

Desi and I walked back to her car.

"See, that wasn't too bad," she said as she snapped her seat belt closed.

I rested my head against the back of the seat. "No, not too bad. And at least I was able to talk to Drew about the design plans. If she had any, my life will be so much easier."

"Do you want me to tag along when you go to his

house?" she asked. "I can help you look. I do owe you for coming with me to this."

I smiled at her. "Sure. I have too much work to catch up on today for other events, but I was thinking about going tomorrow."

"Works for me." She drove me back to the Boathouse and dropped me off outside the front door. "See you tomorrow."

I gave her a little wave and walked inside. It was quiet as Beth had taken the kids home with her. She'd even offered to keep them until after dinner so that I'd have a chance to catch up on work. I peeked into the main room, my stomach roiling at the sight of the Halloween decorations. I wasn't going to be able to put off decorating for much longer.

9

*W*hen we stopped by Angela's house the next day, a neighbor's leaf blower heralded our arrival. I parked my car along the sidewalk in front of the house and we got out, just standing there for a minute with our hands in our pockets, neither of us hurrying to approach the door.

"This feels weird." Desi stared at Angela's house.

"It does." I let my eyes dart to the gate to the backyard and shivered. Last time we'd been here, a body had fallen out of a sarcophagus. That was enough to scare anyone away from the house. In fact, I wouldn't be surprised if the neighborhood kids started rumors about the witch who lived in this house.

With the fog drifting in off the water and surrounding the house, it struck me again how perfect this house was for Halloween. I half expected to see a bat fly out of an upper window or spot a ghost in the attic. Actually, I was surprised that Angela hadn't wanted to keep the haunted house at her residence, but perhaps her ideas grew too big for a single house and neighborhood to comfortably manage.

We walked up the concrete walkway to the front door. Someone in the neighborhood must have been burning wood in their fireplace because the air reeked of woodsmoke. Before I could even rap on the door, it opened.

"How did you know we were here?" Desi asked.

Drew gestured with thumb at a blinking light in the corner of the porch roof. "The camera notifies me if anyone approaches the house."

My eyes fixed on the blinking light. "Did the police check the footage from the day Mindy died?"

He nodded. "They did, but it didn't show anything. The backyard gate is too far over there." He pointed to the side. "Angela always wanted me to install another camera over there, but I hadn't done it yet." He sighed. "Now I wish I had." He looked at us. "Are you here to look for the haunted house designs?"

"Yes. Is now a good time?" I asked.

"As good as any, I guess. I've been having a difficult time staying focused on work with everything that's been going on." He motioned for us to enter the house, closing the door behind us.

The inside of the Laveaux house was filled with artwork —paintings on the walls, sculptures in every corner, and decorative chandeliers hanging from the ceiling. Next to me, I heard Desi suck in her breath as she took it all in as well.

Drew caught us looking at the art and laughed. "Angela considers our home to be her own personal art gallery. Actually, this is the house she grew up in, so we're surrounded by her family heirlooms as well as the more modern pieces she's chosen."

"It's beautiful," I said truthfully. While there was an abundance of art, somehow, in Angela's house, it didn't feel forced.

"Thank you." He led us down a hallway to a back room and turned the old-fashioned brass doorknob. "This is Angela's studio. If she had any, the design plans would be in there."

"Thank you."

He flipped on the overhead light and stepped aside. Desi and I entered the room, halting in the entrance. Just like the rest of her house, this room was covered in art, some still in progress in the back of the room and some showcased throughout the space. Materials for new projects lay in haphazard stacks on every available surface.

"I'll be right down the hall if you need me." He disappeared from view.

"Where do we start?" Desi asked, her eyes wide.

"I don't know." This wasn't going to be an easy task. "How about we start with the desk? Maybe she left it there."

Desi started to sort through all of the items on top of the desk. I moved around to the other side of the large wooden desk and opened up a file drawer. Neat folders held bills and such, but much to my dismay, the plans weren't there. I pushed the door shut and sighed.

"I take it you didn't find anything in there." Desi raised her eyebrows at me. "I sure didn't. How does one person have so much stuff?"

"Nope. Now what?" The idea of going through all of her stacks was daunting, but I couldn't picture her storing it somewhere where it could get lost.

Desi surveyed the space, pointing at the back wall. "You look through that stuff and I'll take this half of the room."

I nodded.

An hour later, Desi said, "You'll never believe what I just found."

I poked my head up from the file drawer I was looking through. "What is it?"

She held up a paper-wrapped object, waving it slightly in the air.

"Ok?" I still had no clue what it was, but judging by the stunned expression on Desi's face, it must be something big.

She peeled the paper back, revealing a stack of green paper. "It's forty thousand dollars."

Files slid off my lap and onto the floor as I stood quickly. "Forty thousand dollars? Are you sure?"

"Uh huh. I counted it. There's forty bundles of a thousand dollars each."

I grabbed it from her. "That's got to be fake, right? A prop for something?"

"I don't know, those one hundred-dollar bills look pretty real to me."

I examined the money and handed it back to her. "I'm no expert, but those look real to me too. Who keeps that much cash in lying around their office?"

Desi shrugged. "Angela, I guess. Maybe she's paranoid about the banks crashing or something. I don't think I've ever seen that much money in person, much less keep it in a drawer."

"Where did you find it?"

She pointed at a file cabinet in the corner of the room. "In the bottom drawer of that cabinet."

"Is there more than that?"

"No. Just that."

"Well, put it back. She would probably be angry if she knew we found it."

Desi complied. "That's weird though, right? To keep that much cash in the house?"

"Maybe it's common for wealthy people to do. I mean,

seriously, look at this place. Angela's family must have done well for themselves."

"Yeah. After seeing this place, I'm curious about them. I'll have to find out what her maiden name was and ask Mom if they have any information about the family down at the historical society." She glanced around the room, as if suddenly remembering why we were there. "We've already been here over an hour. Let's find those plans and get out of here."

Another hour later, we sat in the middle of the floor, empty-handed.

"Argh." I looked around. "How is it not here?"

"Maybe she has it with her," Desi answered.

"At the jail?" She might have a point though. Every time I'd seen Angela, she'd carried a large purse. She could have kept any plans in there.

I slumped against the side of the desk. "Now what? How am I going to get it back from her?"

"I don't know. Maybe Drew can get it if they let him see her." She peered at me. "Are you sure she had some sort of written plans for the haunted house?"

"I'm pretty sure she must have. There were too many details and she's so particular that I can't imagine she wouldn't have them written down." I pushed myself off the ground and held out a hand to her, to help her to standing. I looked around, grimacing. "Now I owe you. Lunch at the Thai restaurant in Everton?"

Her eyes lit up. "Yum. You know I love that place."

I grinned. "Me too. Let's find Drew and then we can leave."

We followed the sound of soft classical rock to a room just down the hall. Drew sat at a modern metal desk, staring at his computer.

"Whoa. This is really different than Angela's studio," Desi whispered.

"No kidding." The dark hardwood floors in Drew's office were shiny and free of clutter. A lone painting that looked like something Mikey had done hung on his wall. I was pretty sure it was worth quite a bit more than the drawings taped to our refrigerator door. Unlike Angela's, his desk held nothing but a computer keyboard and monitor.

I cleared my throat and he looked up.

"Did you find what you were looking for?"

I shook my head. "We didn't. I think she may have the designs with her, if she had already created them. Do you know if you'll be able to see her soon? Maybe you could check with the police to see if you can get them back or at least find out what she had in mind?"

He stood from behind his desk. "I'll check with them today. I know how important the haunted house is to Angela." His face paled. "This must be devastating for her, not being able to manage the event. She lives for Halloween every year."

I smiled softly at him. "I'll do everything I can to make this event a success, and I'm sure they'll release her soon."

"I hope so." He fiddled with a piece of paper on her desk and then looked up at me. "I'm sure she didn't kill Mindy."

"I'm sure you're right." I looked at Desi, but she was checking out an antique oil painting on the wall. Should I tell him about the cash? It wasn't like Angela had locked the file drawer or anything, so he probably already knew about it. "We did come across something though."

"What?" He cocked his head to the side.

"Forty thousand dollars in cash. We left it where we found it, in the bottom drawer of that file cabinet against the back wall. I thought you should know. Maybe it should be locked up in a safe or something?" It occurred to me that they probably had some sort of safe in this house, with all of the valuable items.

He leaned against his desk and ran his finger through his hair. "Forty thousand dollars? In cash?"

I nodded.

"I don't know where she got that kind of money from. Most of what we have is tied up in investments and can't be quickly liquidated. In fact, that's why I'm having problems posting the two million dollar bail they're requesting."

My jaw dropped. Two million dollar bail?

"But all that money. Could Mindy have been right?" He shook his head. "No, it's impossible."

I gave him a sharp look. "What did Mindy say?"

"It's nothing." He waved his hand. "I shouldn't have said anything while Angela isn't even here to defend herself."

"Drew. What if whatever it is was why Mindy was killed?"

He sighed. "Fine. Mindy came to the house one day accusing Angela of embezzling money from the MUMs group. Of course, I didn't want to believe it and Angela denied taking any money, so Mindy dropped it. But now with that money you've found, I don't have an explanation for where it came from. So ..."

"So the money we found could be stolen?" I asked.

He reddened. "I'm not saying that. More likely, it's money Angela hid away in case of an emergency. Her family had a history of not trusting the government and we've found stashes of money squirreled away all over this house."

By this time, Desi was listening intently. "Did you tell the police about this?"

"No!" he said. "I'm not going to tell the police that the woman they think my wife murdered was accusing her of embezzlement." He shook his head vigorously. "It's probably all a big mistake. Angela would never kill anyone. Jill ..." He hesitated. "You have some experience with things like this, right?"

"Uh. Like what?"

"You know, murder investigations. Angela mentioned to me one time that you'd solved a murder while you were on vacation last month."

"She did?" I hadn't thought Angela knew much about me, or cared to know much about me, but perhaps Beth had said something to her about what happened to us at the lake.

"She always knows everything there is to know about the people she works with." He laughed. "If you hadn't noticed, she's a bit of a control freak. Truth be told, the reason she told me about it was because she was upset you weren't in town to assist her with the haunted house that week."

I smiled. "I'm sure she's just concerned about the event."

"She's like that with everything." He looked past Desi to the hallway. "If you hadn't guessed, this is the only room in the house that's actually mine." He made a face. "But I know my wife and she didn't kill Mindy. Maybe you could find something out?"

Desi and I exchanged glances.

"We'll do our best," I said.

He ushered us out of the house and when we were in my minivan, Desi turned to me.

"So, we're investigating this now? Tomàs is going to kill me if he finds out."

"I never said we were investigating it. Maybe just asking a few questions to help lead the police to the real killer." I felt a flush rising up my neck and I started the car.

"Uh huh." She laughed. "I've heard that before." In a

69

quieter voice, she asked, "Do you really think Angela is innocent?"

I stared straight ahead at the road as I drove. "I do. There's no way she would have let anything interfere with the Ericksville Haunted House. After all these years of managing it, it's become a big deal and it's her reputation on the line."

"I think you're right. I'll ask around at the MUMs leadership meeting. Maybe someone there knows something about the relationship between Angela and Mindy."

I turned to smile at her. "Thanks, Desi. I owe you."

"Yep. I'm getting spring rolls and pad thai when we get to the restaurant. Maybe even a Thai iced tea."

I grinned to myself. Desi and I would do a little sleuthing, but this wasn't going to turn into a full-blown investigation. That, I didn't have time for if I wanted to pull off the haunted house in a fashion that wouldn't make Angela Laveaux come after me as soon as she was released from prison. On second thought, maybe it wasn't such a good idea to try to figure out what had really happened to Mindy. The world might be better off with Angela behind bars.

"You don't really think that do you?" Desi asked in horror as I pulled into a parking space at Tasty Thai.

"What?" I turned off the engine and stared at her. "Think what?"

"That Angela should remain behind bars."

My face reddened. "Oh. I didn't realize I said that out loud." I sighed. "No, of course not. I'll do what I can to get her out of jail." I opened my car door. "Now, let's eat some yummy food and forget about all of this for a while, ok?"

"No argument here."

10

-----

*W*hen I arrived home that day after a late evening at work, Adam was sitting on the couch. The TV was turned on, but he wasn't watching it. Instead, he was staring at a spreadsheet on his computer. Worry lines crossed his forehead. He was so engrossed in what he was doing that he didn't notice my approach. Goldie lay at his feet, only looking up for a moment when I entered the room.

I rested my hand on his shoulder. "Hey."

"Hi." He glanced at me, turned off the TV and patted the cushion next to him.

"How were the kids? Did you have dinner?" When I'd passed the kitchen, I'd caught a whiff of macaroni and cheese, but he'd cleaned up all of the mess. I'd eaten my leftover Thai food for dinner at my desk.

He nodded. "Mac 'n' cheese. They both liked it. I got them to bed about an hour ago."

"Good." I stepped over his feet and sat down next to him on the couch, pulling my legs up under me as I turned to face him. "What's going on? You look worried."

He sighed and shut the lid to the laptop. "I don't think we're going to be able to go to Disneyland next summer."

My heart sunk. Adam and I had been discussing a Disney trip for the last month and I'd really looked forward to going. Luckily, I hadn't told Mikey about it yet. I'd learned that with young kids, it was best to not tell them anything until close to the date you were actually leaving as they didn't have much of a concept of time anyway. That alone saved me from countless repetitions of "Are we going tomorrow?"

"Oh." I peered at him. "Why not?"

He sighed and leaned back against the couch cushions. "It's too expensive. My practice isn't in the black yet and we just can't afford it."

I nodded. "Ok."

Starting a solo law practice had been a much more expensive endeavor than we'd anticipated, but I still believed it had been the right decision for our family.

He ran his fingers through his hair. "I'm sorry, honey. I know how much you were looking forward to it."

"Yeah, I was, but I understand. Besides, maybe we can go next year when Ella's older and can enjoy it more. Mikey will be thrilled whenever we end up going." I'd always known there was a possibility we wouldn't be able to go that year and I didn't want to jeopardize our finances to do so.

He smiled at me. "Thanks. I would have liked to do it too. Maybe we can reassess the trip in the spring."

I bit my lip. "How are we doing otherwise—financially?" Me going back to work had allowed Adam to quit his demanding corporate job, but working at the Boathouse paid less than half of what I'd made at my old marketing job in Seattle. "Do I need to find a different job?" I was finally feeling like I'd hit my stride with my event coordinator job and I hoped I wouldn't have to leave it.

"No. I think we're fine for now." He tapped his fingers on the metallic lid. "We have savings and I'm sure things will pick up at my office. In the meantime, I don't want to dip into our savings too much unless we have to."

He looked at me. "You know, there is one thing. When I was going over our receipts, I noticed we've been spending a lot at the grocery store."

I tipped my head to the side. "I don't feel like we've been spending any more than usual." I tried to not buy things we didn't need at the store and although I'd been buying more pre-chopped veggies and such because I'd been working more, I figured it evened out because we weren't wasting food.

He opened the lid on his laptop again, tapped the mouse pad a few times, and pulled up a detailed spreadsheet. My eyes widened. He must have recorded every single individual item from all of our grocery receipts from the past three months. He needed some clients ASAP.

He poked a finger at a bolded figure at the bottom. "See, that's how much we spent on groceries last month."

I bent down to look at it and then straightened. The total was about what I'd expected.

"Uh huh."

"Before we were married, I spent about a fifth of that on my monthly grocery bill. I think we can definitely cut down on this expense."

I looked at him like he was crazy and I had a hard time keeping my voice level when I replied. "Ok, let me get this straight. You're comparing our grocery bill now with two adults, a preschooler, a baby, and two pets to what you spent

73

as a twenty-something? All you ate back then was ramen. That's not healthy."

"I didn't have ramen noodles every night," he said indignantly. "When I lived in that house with roommates, we made dinner most nights. But it cost nothing near what we're spending now."

I shut my mouth and counted to ten, not speaking to him until I was calmer. "We have to buy food for us, which is more expensive now that you're home full-time, snacks for Mikey, formula and diapers for Ella, and food for Goldie and Fluffy. Plus, that was seven years ago. Grocery costs are rising like crazy every year. Our bill is bound to be more expensive than when you were living the single life." I put my index finger to my lips. "Hey, idea—how about you shop for groceries next time? That way you can try and lower our grocery bill." I smiled sweetly at him.

He brightened. "That's a great idea. I'll make a list on the spreadsheet right now. I peeked at the ads for this week and it looks like if I go to four different stores, I'll be able to save us a few dollars." He leaned forward and kissed my cheek. "If you don't mind, I'm going to work on some things in my office until bed."

I tried to remind myself that my husband was concerned about our overall finances and probably hadn't meant to accuse me of wasting our grocery money. Plus, I knew he'd come home with all the wrong things or impulse buys that we didn't really need in the house.

"No problem. I have some things to do too."

I watched him walk down the hall to his office. Goldie hopped up on the couch next to me, taking Adam's place. He and I sat in silence for a few minutes, with me running my fingers across his silky fur. Adam was normally pretty calm, a go-with-the-flow kind of guy. Seeing him so upset about this made my anxiety over our finances increase.

I knew all small businesses had rough patches and it would be a while before his practice reached profitability, but it was worrisome nonetheless. Had we made the right decision for him to leave his high-paying job? Living in the Seattle area wasn't cheap and many families had to have two incomes just to make ends meet.

I glanced at a photo hanging over the mantel. Desi had caught Adam, me, and the kids enjoying some family time out in the sun on our trip to Eastern Washington in August. No, it had definitely been the right decision even if it meant tightening our belts. If Adam had stayed at his old job, we'd never have gone on that vacation. He'd regularly forfeited vacation time each year because of his workload. Goldie nudged my hand, alerting me that that I'd stopped petting him. I moved my hand over his fur and he settled back down.

I felt selfish for complaining about how stressful my job had been lately with the haunted house being such a fiasco. We were fortunate to have a family business that I could step into. Plus, although I hadn't been sure of it in the beginning, it was actually a perfect fit for me, even if I had to deal with clients like Angela.

I'd had my share of both difficult clients and coworkers in my previous marketing position too—it wasn't something unique to my current job. Back when I worked in the corporate world, I'd had a boss that treated all of the female employees like they were only there to get his coffee and gave all of the best assignments to the men. That had been a rough six months until he'd been transferred to another branch.

In comparison, Angela's antics were nothing. If I could

just make it through Halloween, the future would be a little brighter. Maybe by then, Adam would have a few more clients and our finances wouldn't be as tight.

~

Later that week, Desi and I attended another MUMs event, a mommy and me yoga class at the community center. We'd each been partnered with another MUM to do some of the exercises.

After coming out of a downward dog that had turned into more of a wandering dog as I chased after a crawling Ella, I'd returned to our seat on the floor next to a woman about my age. She smiled at me.

"Oh my goodness, your daughter is so beautiful. All that red hair," she gushed. She glanced at me. "And I see where she gets it from. What I wouldn't give to have hair that color naturally." She held up a lock of her own hair, which was a lovely shade of dark brown.

I smiled at her. "Thank you. It runs in my family." It never failed to amaze me how fascinated strangers were with Ella's red curls. I wondered if my mom had gone through the same thing with me when I was a baby. "How old is your little girl?" I motioned to the baby she held in her arms.

She tilted the child to face me. "Daphne's a Christmas baby, so about ten months old. And yours?" Her daughter was wearing a beautifully crocheted unicorn cap.

"She turns one in a few days. I'm Jill, and this is Ella." I positioned Ella in front of me and handed her a ball that I'd pulled out of the diaper bag. I'd had my doubts, but this MUMs group was turning out to be more fun than I'd thought. It was nice being around other moms with children the same age as mine, and I was again grateful that I had a flexible job that would allow me to pop out of the office for the afternoon to spend time with my daughter.

I loved that Desi had kids around the same age as mine, but I needed to meet new people with kids too. All of my former co-workers and many of my old friends were childless, so it seemed like every year I lost touch with more and more of them as our lives went in different directions.

She beamed at me. "I'm Maria. It's nice to meet you."

I held tight to Ella as she fought to squirm away from me. "Where did you get that gorgeous hat? I've seen other babies wearing them. Did you all get them from the same place?"

She pointed at Lisa. "Lisa makes them. Aren't they wonderful?"

"She makes all of those? I wish I was that talented," I said wistfully. I'd tried to crochet a blanket when Mikey was a baby, but it had turned out rather lopsided.

"Me too. It takes her days to make each one of them." In a quieter voice, she said, "I guess that's why she can get away with charging so much for them." She rearranged Daphne's hat.

"Are you guys talking about the hats?" Desi came over with Lina and looked from Maria to me.

"Maria was just telling me that Lisa is the one who makes these. Apparently she has a business making them." I turned to Maria. "This is my sister-in-law, Desi, and her daughter, Lina."

They exchanged pleasantries.

"So you're telling me that Lisa made all of the hats the babies here are wearing?" Desi asked, her eyes wide. "That's a lot of work."

77

Maria looked around at the other attendees. "Yes, looks like it."

"Have you been a member of this MUMs group for long?" I asked. "Desi and I just joined a couple of weeks ago, but it's been fun so far."

She nodded vigorously. "Oh, yes, I was one of the founding members of the group since Daphne was born fairly early in the year."

"So you've known Lisa for a while?" Desi asked.

Maria nodded again. "She's been our leader since we started. She's great, isn't she? So full of energy." She shook her head. "I don't know how she does it all."

I glanced at Lisa. Her blonde hair hung in perfect waves down her back as she held her baby up while doing the Warrior Two position. It must have taken hours in the gym and in MUMs stroller groups to achieve her slim physique.

"No kidding." I chased after Ella. At this rate, I'd have a slim figure soon without stepping foot in a gym. She'd be walking soon and then I'd really have to run to keep up with her when she took off.

"Did you ever meet Mindy?" Desi asked.

"No," Maria said. "But I heard what happened to her. How awful. Lisa was really shaken up about it. I'm glad I wasn't there that day. I'd planned to come and help move the Halloween decorations, but Lisa called me and said they didn't need any more help."

I stared at her. Didn't need any more help? It seemed odd that Lisa would have told her that because the shed had been packed with decorations for the haunted house.

"Had you been to Angela's house before?" Desi stuck Lina on a blanket for some tummy time. Lina looked up at us as if she were in pain and promptly laid her head down to the side to fall asleep. "Her house is gorgeous."

"I've been there one time," Maria said. "Angela isn't usually very friendly with the women in the local MUMs groups, but for some reason, she offered up her house for the group picnic last summer." She looked toward Lisa. "Lisa organized it, but Angela let us have it on a beautiful spot of lawn overlooking the water. She wouldn't let anyone in the house though."

So, Lisa had been to Angela's house before and would be familiar with the backyard.

"Did Lisa and Mindy ever argue?" I let Ella wander a few feet away and then stood to get her.

Maria laughed. "What, do you think Lisa killed Mindy or something?"

Desi and I looked at each other before I scooped Ella up.

Maria stopped laughing. "You've got to be kidding me. Lisa would never do that. She and Mindy always got along. Now if it were Angela that was murdered, that might have been a different story. Everyone had spats with her." She stood. "I'd better get home. My husband will be home soon and I need to start dinner." She picked up Daphne and walked away with her.

"So we may not be her favorite people," I said to Desi.

"No kidding. Perhaps we should be a little more subtle if we're going to ask the MUMmys more questions."

"MUMmys?" I smiled.

She shrugged. "It sounded appropriate. But I'm serious. I like this group and I don't want to jeopardize any of the friendships we're forming, so let's try to keep any sleuthing on the down-low."

"Fine with me. From everything you've said and what I've witnessed, none of the MUMs seem to know much about Mindy anyway." I checked my watch. "Maria was right. It's getting late and we've got to pick up Mikey and

Anthony from preschool. Do you want me to grab Anthony and drop him off at the café while you close up?"

"That would be great." She made a face. "I like getting involved with other moms, but I'd forgotten how much effort it takes to make and keep friends."

"No kidding." I put Ella in her stroller and waved at Desi. "I'll see you soon with Anthony."

"Bye."

11

The next day, I was at work and everything seemed to be going wrong with the haunted house, starting with the additional decorations Angela had ordered a few weeks ago.

"There's more in the truck, right?" I eyed the small cardboard box the delivery driver held out to me.

"Nope. This is it, ma'am."

"There were supposed to be five large boxes of cobwebs, not one tiny box."

He shrugged. "I don't know what to tell you. I only deliver them and this is all that's on my manifest."

I took the box and set it down while I signed for the delivery. His truck's engine roared as he jetted off to his next stop, leaving a trail of exhaust that lingered just above the asphalt in the parking lot.

I stared at the box, wondering what I was going to do. This definitely wasn't enough to cover all of the main room of the Boathouse. I may not have had the details of Angela's plan for the haunted house, but I clearly remembered her saying she'd ordered enough cobwebs for the whole thing.

What was I going to do? This was going to be the worst haunted house Ericksville had ever seen.

I moved the box into the event space near the decorations the police had returned to us after they concluded their investigation of the shed at Angela's house. I shuddered, thinking about the lid popping off of the sarcophagus, revealing Mindy's body. The police still had the coffin, and I fervently hoped that Angela wouldn't be replacing it. I didn't think I could take having one at the haunted house, although I suppose it would have added another layer of eeriness to the decor.

I gazed at the empty walls and floors. There was less than a week to go before the haunted house opened to the public and I needed to somehow transform this room into a magical destination that would scare the socks off of everyone in Ericksville. Right now, the clean hardwood floors, whitewashed walls, and big windows were more suited to a summer wedding.

A hand touched my shoulder and I whirled around.

"Sorry!" Beth smiled at me. "You're awfully jumpy today."

"I was thinking about the haunted house and perhaps creeping myself out a bit."

"Ah," she said. "Did you decide what you're going to do?"

I shook my head. "No. Halloween is definitely not my strong suit. My family wasn't that into it. I'm going to go online to get some ideas, but I'm sure they won't be up to Angela's standards. I'd hoped she would be able to help, but it looks like that's not going to be anytime soon."

Beth tapped her finger against her chin. "You know, we do know someone who loves Halloween."

I narrowed my eyes at her. "Adam?"

She nodded. "Yep. He always did the displays on our front porch when the kids were young."

Hmm. I wasn't sure how I felt about working alongside my husband at the Boathouse, but I was running out of options.

I sighed. "I'll ask him. Thanks for the suggestion."

"No problem. Remember, if you need me for anything, I'm right down the hall."

I didn't have any events to manage that day, so I'd dressed more casually than normal and actually had pockets to hold my cell phone. I pulled it out of my sweatshirt and called Adam.

"Hi, honey," he answered before I said a word.

"Hi." I paused. "I have a favor to ask of you."

"A favor?" He chuckled. "What kind of favor?"

"You know how I'm working on the Ericksville Haunted House?"

"How could I forget? You've been talking about it nonstop for the last month."

"I haven't been that bad—right?"

"Um, sure. Anyway, what about it?"

I heard him tapping his pen on his desk.

"I was hoping since things aren't too busy at the office, that you might want to help out with it. Angela is still being held at the county jail and I don't know what she wants it to look like."

"But it's in only a week. Some of those things take time, like building a hay maze, or a graveyard, or any number of things."

My mind was spinning. The last haunted house I'd been in had been when I was a teenager, and I didn't remember most of it because I'd been too busy laughing at it all with my friends. I didn't want the teenagers in town to be laughing at our haunted house.

"So can you help with it or not?"

"I can help. There are so many things I'd love to try." He sounded giddy. "When do you want me there?"

"Anytime is good."

"I'll see you in ten minutes." He hung up the phone.

When he got there, he toured the main room, scanning every detail of it as though it was his first time seeing it, not the five hundredth time since he was a kid.

I hung back near the entrance, waiting for him to finish his assessment. The inside of the Boathouse smelled like the chocolate chip cookies Desi had baked that morning. Too bad she hadn't left any in my office before taking them over to the café. With any luck, I'd have time to sneak over there for one before the end of the day.

"Ok. I have some ideas, but I don't know what we have to work with." He scanned the stacks of decorations I'd piled in the corner. "We can use most of it, but we're going to need more."

"What did you have in mind?" I was almost afraid to find out.

"I'm thinking a haunted farm would be fun to do. We can stack hay bales in that corner for a maze, build a barn structure over there, and then maybe have different scenarios representing rooms of the farmhouse like the kitchen or storage areas." He spread his arms wide, enthusiasm spreading from his voice. "Imagine a barn with zombies popping up from the hay, reaching their fingers out to touch you." His eyes gleamed with excitement.

My eyes widened. "Mikey will be terrified."

"Nah, he'll be fine."

"If you say so." Our son still slept with a night-light on in his room, so I was pretty sure zombies would give him night-mares. At least Adam was home now and I could give him the unenviable job of calming Mikey down when he had a nightmare. "How are you going to pull all of that off on such short notice?"

"Hmmm." He stroked his chin as he looked around, echoing the gesture his mother had made earlier that morning in the same spot. "I bet Dad's buddies down at the model train museum would be willing to help out. Some of them are great carpenters and it is for charity."

"And the materials?" I looked dubiously at what we already had. The budget for the haunted house wasn't massive and I'd counted on Angela's expertise to create everything.

He snapped his fingers. "Don't worry about it. I'll figure it all out, ok?"

I shrugged. "Ok. With Angela gone, I've got enough to worry about with the logistics of the event. If you can handle the decorations, I'd be grateful."

"Don't worry about it, honey." He squealed like a little girl seeing a unicorn. "This is going to be so much fun!"

I shook my head. I'd never seen my husband so excited about anything, much less something creative like this.

I stopped by Beth's office on the way back to my own. She was writing something on a yellow notepad.

"I called Adam."

"I thought I heard his voice." She pushed the notepad away from her. "What did he think?"

"He thinks it will be tons of fun to put it together."

She laughed. "He never wanted to be involved with the business because he deemed it boring. It's ironic that now he's excited to be a part of it."

"Yeah. I just hope he can get it all done in time. If you

see Lincoln, give him a heads up that Adam wants to enlist the help of the volunteers down at the train museum and historical society to help with the event."

She laughed. "Will do." She peered more closely at me. "How is everything else going? Did the event ad get placed in the newspaper? Have the signs been printed?"

"Yes. I checked those off my list last week."

"I'm sorry you had to take on all of the extra work for this event. Who would have expected Angela to get arrested for murder? The woman is obnoxious, but I didn't think she had it in her to kill someone. Actually, when you told me about finding a body at her house, I was surprised that it wasn't hers."

"Me too." I remembered thinking the same thing when the sarcophagus had opened. "But the show must go on." I sighed. "If we don't have the best haunted house this town's ever seen, we'll never live it down. Angela made a big deal to the Chamber of Commerce about it being here this year."

"I know. And it would be bad for business if it fails." She scrunched up her face. "Although, I was going over our bookings for November and December and we're filling up quickly. We're going to have a busy holiday season with all of those company parties."

Ugh. One more seasonal stressor to worry about. At least this year, I wouldn't be obligated to attend Adam's company party.

"Will we have more staff to help?" At the end of the summer, many of the seasonal staff had left for other jobs or to return to college.

"Yes. A couple of our waiters and event staff will be home from college for Christmas, so we'll have some assistance with things." She eyed me. "It's going to be busy though, Jill. I'll probably assign a few of the company parties to you to manage. Are you up for it?"

I smiled brightly at her. "Of course." I laughed. "At the moment, I just need to make it through Halloween."

"Let me know if you need help, ok?"

"I will. I think with Adam on the job, I have everything under control at the moment."

She gave me a thumbs-up and I exited her office, returning to my desk to check off a few more things from my to-do list. As much as I hoped Angela would be back soon, I needed to prepare for the possibility that she wouldn't. There had been a MUMs event that day that I hadn't been able to attend, but Desi had planned to be there. I hoped she'd been able to do some subtle snooping among the other moms. I finished a few more things and headed over to the café for an afternoon pick-me-up.

12

*W*hen I arrived at the café I didn't see Desi. The afternoon crowds had dissipated, but there was a group of moms in the back of the café, chatting as their children played with the assortment of toys. A few students were holed up with their computers, sitting on stools at the bar positioned against a side wall.

I ordered my coffee and scone and asked her assistant, Andrea, "Do you know when Desi will be back?"

She checked the clock on the wall. "She should be back soon. She said she planned to the leave the mall in Everton around two thirty so she'd be back by three."

The mall? Why was Desi at a mall? She wasn't normally much of a shopping person.

"Hey, sorry I'm late," Desi said as she breezed in the door. "I had to drop Lina off with Tomàs after the MUMs meeting."

Both Andrea and I stared at her. Her face was covered in makeup better suited for a night out on the town than an afternoon shift at a small-town café.

"Uh, Desi?" Andrea asked. "What happened to your face?"

"What?" Desi touched her cheeks. "Oh, yeah. I'd better go scrub this off."

I followed her to the back of the room where the small one-person bathroom was located.

"What were you and Lina doing?"

"The MUMs and I were at a mom and baby fashion show event at the mall. All the moms got makeovers at the makeup counter and we and our babies were given matching outfits to wear."

I raised an eyebrow. "A fashion show?" Now I was glad that I'd skipped out on it. What was cute on Ella would not be cute on me. It had been a long time since I could get away with wearing bows on my clothes.

She shrugged. "It was surprisingly fun. I've got pictures I can show you later. Anyway, I need to wash this off. Stick around though—I wanted to talk with you about something."

She shut the door on me and I retrieved my coffee and pastry from where I'd left them on the front counter. I settled myself at a table for two overlooking Lighthouse Park. With the cold weather, not many people were out on the lawn, but there were still a few die-hard joggers and dog walkers. The area surrounding the lighthouse was empty; the local historical society offered tours of it on the weekends, but the entrance was gated off during the week.

Desi sat down at my table, her face freshly washed. "Better?"

I smiled. "It didn't look that bad—it just didn't look like you."

"Yeah, they went a little overboard. I had to keep the

woman at the cosmetics counter from putting blush on Lina's cheeks after she was doing with my makeover."

"Whoa. Did the other moms have their babies made up?"

She rolled her eyes. "No. Don't be silly. I know we thought some of the other moms were silly, but most of them are really nice. I even made a coffee date with a couple of them for next week. I'm sure you can come with us if you'd like."

I took a deep breath. She was right. I had gone into joining the group with some preconceptions.

"That's great. When this haunted house mess is over with, I'd love to go to the next meeting." I crossed my fingers in the air. "I promise I'll keep a more open mind."

She grinned. "You weren't completely wrong. Some of them are rather vapid, but they're still nice."

"In all of your friendly chats today, did you find out anything about Angela or Mindy? Were they really friends like Drew said, or did Angela just order her around like she did to everyone else?" I sipped from my coffee, enjoying the freshly roasted beans that Desi bought from a local coffee roaster.

She shook her head. "No, they didn't know too much. I asked around, but most of them had never met Mindy and they weren't big fans of Angela. Apparently she wields an iron fist with the MUMs leaders too—it's not just her haunted house management style. Actually, I found out that Angela's the reason the last treasurer left." She sighed. "If I'd only known when I volunteered for the job."

"I'm not surprised. I have the feeling not many people like her."

"Her husband seems to be devoted to her, so she must

have some good qualities." Desi broke a piece off of my scone and popped it into her mouth.

I pretended not to see her take my treat. "He seems sure that we'll be able to help figure out what really happened to Mindy. I mean, we've accidentally solved a couple of murders, but we're not the police."

"I know." She washed the bite of scone down with some coffee. "But you're getting quite a reputation around here."

"Do you think he really expects you and me to clear Angela's name?"

She shrugged. "Maybe. He does have a point. Since we're involved with the MUMs organization, we do have contact with many of the people that Mindy had in common with Angela. We found her body at Angela's house, so it's probably someone they both knew."

"I guess." I wasn't sure how I felt about getting actively involved in another murder case.

She reached for another piece and I swatted her hand away.

"Mine," I said.

"Hey, I made that." She mock glared at me.

"Then go get your own." I returned the feigned glare. "It was bad enough that all day I had to smell the chocolate chip cookies you made this morning when you didn't have the common courtesy to leave a few in the kitchen for me."

"Those were for the Harvest Festival. I only had time to make four dozen, so there weren't any extras. If you'd prefer not to bring the full four dozen as your contribution, I can grab one for you to eat now." She raised an eyebrow at me.

I sighed. "No. Thank you for making them. I really do appreciate it. With my luck, Nancy will count them and I don't want to find out what she'll do if she comes up short. I'll have to make do with this scone."

She laughed and retrieved a scone and a cup of coffee for herself.

"I'm starving after that event," she said as she bit into the blueberry scone.

"Was there no lunch offered?"

"They had some sort of tea biscuit and coffee from the espresso stand outside of the store, but the biscuit looked so dry that I couldn't bring myself to try it. I kept imagining all of the goodies in my own bakery case."

"Maybe you should sell your baked goods to them. It sounds like they could use a better supplier."

"Maybe in a year or two." She bit into the scone and chased it with a sip of creamy coffee. "I've got enough to deal with right now. This treasurer thing is harder and more time-consuming than I would have thought."

I laughed. "These volunteer jobs tend to do that. Remember how you warned me away from being the preschool auction chair last year and I didn't listen? You should have taken your own advice."

"There's nothing I can do about it now," she said grumpily. "The other problem is that Mindy never gave me the group's books before she died, so I can't even do my job."

"They're not at the MUMs office?"

"Nope. That's the first place I looked after Lisa told me she'd returned them to Mindy."

"What are you going to do?"

She gave me a puppy dog look. "I was hoping you'd come with me to Mindy's apartment and see if she brought them home. One of the other volunteers gave me Mindy's daughter's phone number. I called her and she said I could stop by tomorrow and take a look. Please? I went to Angela's house with you."

I sighed. "Fine. But I hope you have better luck than I had." If only I'd been able to find the design plans.

"I talked to Mom when I was driving home. She said Adam was helping with the haunted house. Is that true?"

"Unfortunately, yes." I felt a little bad saying that as I was grateful for my husband's help, but there was still a niggling worry at the back of my mind that working together wasn't the best of ideas.

Desi laughed. "Don't worry. I know my brother. He'll be so obsessed with the design for the haunted house that he won't have time to get in your hair."

"I hope so." I finished up my scone and coffee and stood. "Give me a call tonight and we can work out a plan for going to Mindy's house tomorrow."

"Will do. See you later."

I crossed the lawn back over to the Boathouse and ducked my head into the main event space. Adam was pacing the floor muttering something to himself. Well, at least he was engrossed in something. After having him traveling out of state so much for our whole marriage, it was odd having him at home and I was going a little crazy. Moving everything in the cupboards and the loss of TV time to watch my favorite shows were just the tip of the iceberg. Our whole family routine had changed and figuring it out was slow-going. A twinge hit me. Was this how my parents had felt?

Last summer, my parents had announced their separation after almost forty years of marriage. They'd both retired from their teaching jobs and after being home together for a month had decided that they'd be better off apart so they could explore their own interests.

Dad still lived at home, in the basement apartment, and I didn't think either of them was dating anyone. Ugh. That was a horrible thought. It was bad enough for them to split up after all this time, but to date other people? I still held out hope that they'd get back together à la *The Parent Trap*.

All in all, maybe it was good that Adam had this project to work on. And maybe, just maybe, working together wouldn't be so bad.

13

The next day, Desi and I drove to north Everton to see if the financial records for the MUMs group were at Mindy's apartment.

"This is where Mindy lives?" I peered up at the second floor unit in the middle of a large apartment complex.

Desi checked the note she'd typed out on her phone. "D-245. Yep, this is right."

Somebody was moving all of Mindy's things out of her apartment. The door to the unit was open, but not in a scary, someone's-broken-in kind of way. There were boxes piled up along both sides of the hallway and I could hear someone clomping around inside. We looked at each other. If this was Mindy's place, we'd arrived just in time.

"It seems a little soon to be taking her stuff out. I mean, her funeral was only five days ago," I whispered. "Do you think Stacey's having to do it all by herself?"

"I don't know. It does seem soon, but I guess they need everything out before the end of the month or they get stuck with another month's rent."

A man came around the corner, carrying a small box. It

must have been full of books or something, because he lowered it carefully to the top of a stack and then stretched his arms out to the side and flexed his fingers.

"Hi." He cocked his head to the side. "Can I help you with something?"

Desi took the lead. "I'm from the local MUMs group and Stacey Stevens mentioned she'd be here to let me in so I could take a look for a ledger that Mindy had." She looked past him. "Is she here?"

He shook his head. "I don't know about any ledger and Stacey isn't here. Which," he scoffed, "is not a surprise. I'm Joseph Danvers." He jutted his chin in the direction he'd come from. "You're welcome to come back to the office and see what you can find. I haven't packed up everything in that room yet. But if it's already been packed up, you're going to have to wait until it gets to the storage unit. Stacey has a key to it. I've wasted enough time on all of Mindy's junk as is."

Desi and I exchanged surprised looks. Whoever he was, this guy was a real piece of work. The woman had just died and he was complaining about how much stuff she had.

We dutifully followed him back to a room that Mindy had set up as a home office. Her desk appeared untouched and I gave Desi a covert thumbs-up. She grinned back at me. The man left, and with him the tension that had followed him into the room.

"Who was that guy? I remember him from the funeral." I knelt down on the plush beige carpeting next to the desk's bottom drawers, thinking about Mindy's funeral. He'd been the man at the front who didn't look too broken up about Mindy's death—the one who Stacey had glared at. So what was he doing moving Mindy's things out of the apartment?

"I don't know. I've never seen him before. His last name is Danvers, so maybe he's her brother?" Desi pointed at the desk. "Let's get going on this before he decides it's time to pack all of this up too."

We rummaged through the drawers, but even though there were many color-coded files bearing the names of local utilities and banks, we couldn't find any information about the MUMs accounts.

Desi sat back on her heels and shoved some stray strands of hair back from her forehead. "Nothing. The ledger wasn't at the office and it's not here. Where is it?"

I looked around at the boxes. "Maybe it's already been packed?"

"Could be. But how are we supposed to find it then?"

"I don't know."

"I really wish I hadn't volunteered to be treasurer." Desi pouted.

We pushed the drawers in and walked toward the door to the room. Suddenly, Desi stopped in the doorway.

"Hey," I said as I ran into her.

She held a finger up to her mouth. "Shh."

I stopped what I was doing and listened. The man was on the phone with someone and he didn't sound happy. With every word he spoke, his voice increased in volume.

"What do you mean the insurance payout will be delayed? I'm her husband and I'm her beneficiary." He listened intently as the other person spoke. "This is unacceptable. I want to talk with your manager."

Desi and I looked at each other. Her eyes were as wide as mine felt. He was Mindy's husband? That poor woman. The man continued to berate the customer service representatives at the insurance company, and we snuck out of there before he could take his wrath out on us.

When we were down the stairs and to our car, which was parked one building over, Desi said, "So that was Mindy's soon-to-be ex-husband." She held her keys out and beeped the car open.

"Why do you think he's going to be an ex? I mean, I wouldn't want to be married to him, but he told the insurance company he was her husband," I said as I grabbed the door handle.

Desi shrugged. "Angela knows everything and she told me that Mindy was going through a bitter divorce."

"She was gossiping about Mindy?" I asked.

"No, not gossiping. She was complaining about Mindy's unstable personal life and how it was affecting her."

Now it made sense. I hadn't seen Angela as someone who enjoyed the camaraderie of a gossip session, but griping to someone about how another person's misfortune was affecting her—that seemed about right.

"It sounded like she never changed the insurance policy before she died and he gets all of the money," I said.

"That's what I thought too. I bet her daughter isn't happy about that."

"Wouldn't she be ok with her dad getting the money?"

Desi turned the key in the ignition and warm air puffed out of the vent. "He's not her dad. Her parents split up a long time ago. Apparently Stacey never got along with her stepfather."

Angela really did know everything about everyone, just as her husband had claimed.

"That explains the crack he made about Stacey not being here."

"Yeah, he really doesn't seem to like Stacey," Desi said. "Which explains why Stacey isn't here. She probably wanted to stay as far away as possible from her stepfather and figured he could help us find the ledgers just as easily as she could."

"So Mindy had a soon-to-be ex-husband who now inherits her life insurance policy. Sounds like a motive for murder to me," I said.

"But how would he have access to Angela's backyard? That's what strikes me as odd. I wouldn't think he was familiar with her house and I'd assume Mindy would have noticed him following her." Desi bit her lip in thought.

"I don't know. Are you going to call her daughter to find out where the storage unit is?" I asked.

"Yeah, I guess so." She pulled out her phone and tapped a few buttons.

"Hello?" Desi said.

A woman's tinny voice came through the phone line.

"This is Desi Torres. I spoke to you earlier about needing to find the MUMs financial ledger." She listened as the woman spoke. "Uh huh. It wasn't in your mom's apartment. I'm sorry to bother you about this, but I really need the ledger. Do you know where it might be? Your mother's husband was there and he said you had the key to the storage unit." She held the phone away from her ear as the woman's voice became louder. "Ok, we'll see you then."

"What did she say?"

"She wants me to meet her on Sunday at Lindstrom's department store in the mall. She's working today, but doesn't have the storage unit key with her, so she said Sunday would be better." Desi chuckled. "She had a few choice words to say about her mother's former husband."

That explained why Desi held the phone away from her ear. There was definitely no love lost between Stacey and John.

I shrugged. "If you want me to come with you, Sunday works for me. Adam will be home to watch the kids."

Desi gave me a grateful smile. "Thanks, Jill. I really hope

it's there so I can get started on the treasurer work. If it's not, I don't know what I'll do."

I patted her hand. "I'm sure it'll be there."

"Are you going to the Harvest Carnival tonight?" Desi asked. "Anthony's excited about dressing up for it and getting to wear his Halloween costume early."

I nodded. "Mikey too. I hope Adam has their costumes ready. I haven't tried on my Leia get-up. I have my fingers crossed that it'll fit."

She laughed. "Well, you'll recognize me. I'll be wearing my pumpkin costume for the third year in a row. I'm determined to get my money's worth out of that thing. Lina's going to be my baby pumpkin this year."

"Cute."

She dropped me back off at my house a little after one o'clock. Just enough time for a nap with the kids before it would be time to get ready for the Harvest Carnival. Worrying about murderers and their possible motives had worn me out and had kept me from sleeping the night before. With the hope of a little nap, I was looking forward to a fun evening out with my family.

14

"*A*re you ready?" Adam poked his head into our bathroom and whistled. "You look great."

I shot him an amused expression and glanced at my reflection in the mirror. I'd found a loose white dress at a thrift store and tied it with a sash at my waist, then wound my long red hair up into twin buns on either side of my head.

"You look just like Leia." He couldn't stop staring.

"Ok, ok." I turned and took in his costume. He was garbed in a Luke Skywalker costume, complete with light saber. "You know Mikey's going to want one of those, right?"

He grinned at me devilishly. "I know. Why do you think I picked up an extra one?" From behind our dresser, he pulled out another light saber. "We're going to have epic battles."

I laughed. It was good to see him having fun with the kids. Speaking of the kids …

"Are the kids dressed?"

"They are." He left the room and returned with Ella, who'd been turned into an Ewok. "Mikey, get in here."

A miniature Darth Vader entered the room, solemnly saying, "Luke, I am your Father." He then burst into an uncontrollable fit of giggles. "I'm Daddy's father, heeheehee."

I rolled my eyes. This ought to be an interesting Harvest Carnival at the preschool.

"Ok, let's go." I picked up the bottom of my dress and led them down the stairs and the door to the sidewalk.

"You don't want to drive?" Adam asked.

"No." I looked up at the sky. Clouds drifted across the inky darkness, blocking the half moon. "It's a nice night and, besides, there won't be any parking anywhere near the school."

He shrugged. "Ok then." He grabbed the stroller I'd left outside earlier and plopped Ella into it. Her eyes were as wide as half dollars as she looked between her family members.

I kissed her on the forehead as her head was covered by a brown cape and furry ears. "It's ok, sweetie. It's just us."

She examined me dubiously and tugged at the fur on her head.

"Let's go. I don't want to be late." Adam pushed the stroller down the hill toward town.

I had to stifle a laugh. I'd never seen him so excited about a school event before. If only this excitement could translate into the weeks we were required to be parent helpers. I'd be happy to let him have my shift at the preschool so I could avoid Nancy Davenport.

"I'm sure there will be plenty of candy left by the time we get there." I walked carefully on the pavement, holding up my white dress so it wouldn't drag and get dirty.

"Candy?" Mikey asked. "Cool! I'm going to get so much

candy." He put his hand on the stroller, trying to get Adam to go faster.

This was how the Halloween madness began—one piece of candy at a time. The crisp autumn air felt good on my face and we were walking fast enough that I didn't feel cold without a coat. Besides, growing up in the Pacific Northwest, I knew enough to plan costumes where I could layer clothing under my costume. I was currently wearing a pair of long underwear and a thermal undershirt beneath my dress. I'd given Adam similar items for him and the kids; so as long as it didn't rain, we would be good to go for a night outside.

When we arrived at the Busy Bees Preschool, the parking lot had been transformed into a wonderland of kid-friendly game booths, a small bouncy house, and even a petting zoo to one side. They'd outdone themselves this year.

Mikey tugged at my sleeve. "Mommy, can we pet the goats?" He couldn't take his eyes away from the petting zoo.

"Sure, honey, but let's get something to eat first." My stomach grumbled. We'd been so busy getting dressed that we hadn't eaten dinner and I'd counted on there being something to decent eat at the Harvest Carnival.

"Looks like there are hot dogs and chips," Adam said, peering over a sea of small children dressed as pumpkins, characters from popular cartoons, and the ever-popular witch and cat costumes.

"No pizza?" I really didn't like hot dogs, but at this point, I was willing to make an exception.

"Doesn't look like it."

We paid our admission and made our way over to the food. He'd been right—only hot dogs were left.

He paid an exorbitant sum for three hot dogs and we

carried them over to the picnic tables covered with orange plastic tablecloths to eat. I opened the refrigerated bag I'd stuck in the bottom of the stroller and took out the bottle I'd prepared for Ella. She took it out of my hand and sucked it down quickly, no warming necessary.

Mikey was only halfway through his food when he said, "There's Case. Can I go play with him?" He pointed to a little boy standing with his mom near the bounce house. Case's mom waved at me and smiled.

"Sure, go ahead." From where we were sitting, I could see all of the carnival and a makeshift fence had been erected around the parking lot, so I didn't think he could get into much trouble by himself.

"Do you think he's going to finish that?" Adam asked, eyeing Mikey's discarded hot dog.

"No, but do you really want to eat after him?" I screwed up my face.

He grabbed the food and moved it over to his plate. "Eh, it's food."

I laughed and helped Ella get the last few drops out of her bottle before gathering up our garbage and disposing of it in the trash bin.

"Ready?" I asked.

He tossed the last bit of hot dog into his mouth and crumpled up his napkin. "Yep. Let's win us some candy."

On the way over to the carnival games, someone tapped me on the shoulder and I turned around.

"Hi," my friend Dorinda said.

Adam motioned to me that he and Ella were going to keep moving toward Mikey.

Dorinda's four-year-old son tugged at her arm. "Mommy, can I go play with Mikey and Case?"

"Sure, go ahead." She nudged him lightly toward the

other kids and he left, the scales on his red dragon costume flashing as he ran.

"So how are things going?" I asked.

"Good. Daniel is enjoying school this year and Ericksville is starting to feel like home. It's been a lot of work managing the business on my own, but we're finally in the black." She shook her head. "I don't mean to speak ill of the dead, but Louis certainly had made a mess of things at Ericksville Espresso before he died. How about you?"

I laughed. "Well, Adam's new practice is still in its infancy, so he's home a lot, which is a challenge. Things are going well at work and we're actually hosting the big haunted house this year." I felt weird complaining about my husband being home too much to Dorinda. Her husband had died about a year ago and she and her son had moved to Ericksville to be closer to her in-laws. Soon after they'd moved here though, her new business partner at an espresso roasting company had been murdered. Not a very nice welcome. I was happy to hear that things were looking up for her and her son.

"Ooh, that sounds fun. Daniel and I will have to attend." She scanned the preschool grounds. "Speaking of Daniel, where is he?"

I looked around. "There." I pointed at the bounce house, where a red dragon was leaping out of the inflatable structure.

She smiled. "Looks like he's having fun."

Daniel took off across the parking lot to where Mikey and Case were standing in line for the fishing booth. Adam and Ella stood nearby and Dorinda and I joined them.

They reached the front of the line and extended a rod behind a tall divider. An unseen person tugged on the line and they pulled it back to examine their 'fish.'

Mikey unclipped it and beamed at us. "I got vampire teeth, Daddy!"

"Whoa," said Case. "That's so cool."

"Yeah, I want one too!" Daniel bounced up and down.

Mikey immediately unwrapped them and inserted the teeth in his mouth. They were meant for a slightly larger child and dwarfed his small lips. He clomped the teeth up and down.

"How are you going to eat Halloween candy with those in?" Adam teased.

Mikey's eyes widened and he dropped them back into his candy bag. "I didn't think of that. Now can we go pet the goats?"

"Sure." I said goodbye to Dorinda and carried our little Ewok baby over to see the goats too. Although we had a cat and a dog, she'd never been around barnyard animals before, so I wasn't sure how she'd react.

While Mikey and Adam petted the goats, I walked around with Ella, pointing at the bunnies and chickens. She lay against me, content to not be on the ground with them, but her eyes followed the animals as they strutted around.

I was watching a particularly cute brown lop-eared bunny nibbling on a bite of hay on the ground when someone tapped me on the shoulder. I froze. I'd seen Nancy over near the goldfish bowl game and I'd done my best to avoid her.

Please, please let this not be her, the evening is going so well. Ella squirmed, probably sensing my dismay.

I turned around to face the person. Appropriately, Nancy was dressed in a floor-length witch costume, complete with pointy hat. A paper broomstick was taped to her black dress.

"Nancy," I said as pleasantly as I could.

Without preamble, she said, "I heard you're now in charge of the annual Ericksville Haunted House."

I relaxed a little. If it wasn't preschool business, she didn't have much say in what I did or didn't do.

"I am. Why?"

"I wanted to make sure you were having a children's section this year. Last year there wasn't any area where small children could go in the haunted house. It was a disgrace."

I wasn't sure what Adam had planned, but we hadn't discussed a children's area and Angela hadn't mentioned anything in her designs either.

"You know, I don't think we are. Maybe that's an idea for next year."

"Next year? This is a community event. There needs to be more inclusion for all the children. I knew several families last year that weren't able to attend because their small children were unable to participate."

I nodded. "I understand your frustration."

Adam and Mikey came up alongside me and an idea popped into my brain.

"Nancy, this is my husband, Adam. Adam, this is Nancy Davenport."

"Nice to meet you," Adam said, extending his hand. "I've heard a lot about you over the years."

I elbowed him in the side, but he just smiled at Nancy.

She shook his hand vigorously. "So nice to finally meet you. I hear you have a new law practice in town. Maybe you'll be able to take part in more of our school activities since your wife is too busy to do so." She stared pointedly at me.

"Nancy, Adam is actually creating the haunted house this year. Perhaps you could speak with him about your ideas." I smiled sweetly at her and grabbed Mikey's hand.

Before either Nancy or Adam could object, Mikey, Ella, and I joined the flow of people moving toward the petting zoo's exit. Part of me felt bad about throwing Adam under the bus with Nancy, but I'd done my share of dealing with her over the years.

Mikey took part in a race with a few of his classmates that involved eating a mini powdered sugar donut from a string. He came in second place, but all the kids received a candy prize, so he was happy.

"Now can we do the fish bowl game?" Mikey pleaded.

"No, I told you. No more fish. We have a cat and a dog. That's enough animals in our house." Besides, after his most recent fish had died, I'd given away the aquarium. My house was blissfully free of fish and I intended for it to stay that way.

"Just one? I promise I'll take care of it."

I looked over at the glass bowls full of small goldfish swimming lazily in water.

"No. Sorry, kid."

"But, Mommy!"

Adam found us, resting his hand on my shoulder as he took in the fish bowl game. "This looks fun. Did Mikey play yet?"

I removed his hand from my shoulder and glared at him. "No fish."

He held his hands in the air. "Ok, no fish."

He turned to Mikey. "Hey, I think I saw a pumpkin painting area. Do you want to do one with me?"

"Yeah!" Mikey exclaimed, the fish quickly forgotten, just the way it would have been if it had made it into our house.

I followed them over to the picnic table where kids and their parents were drawing pictures on pumpkins with paint brushes. I hovered over Adam while he helped Mikey draw R2-D2 on one.

"Not bad," Adam said, admiring their artwork.

Mikey nodded in agreement. "Mine's way better than Case's." He examined his hands, which were covered in black, blue, and white paint.

Adam laughed and pointed at the handwashing station in between the petting zoo and the painting table. "Go get washed up. I think they brought out apple cider and donuts at the food booth."

He pushed himself up from the table, gingerly moving the paint-coated pumpkin to another, smaller table for drying.

"You know, Nancy isn't as bad as you made her out to be."

I said nothing, bouncing Ella in my arms.

"She had some great ideas for the haunted house. I think we can totally make a separate kids area that will have the same exit as the scarier main section. They can enter through one of the side doors." He was practically bouncing as much as Ella.

He shook his head. "The way you always talked about her, I thought she would be a total monster, but she was really sweet to me."

I pressed my lips together, trying not to scream in the middle of the kids' carnival. "She and I don't always see eye to eye."

"Understood, but maybe she isn't as bad as you think. You do have small kids in common, after all." He nodded to Nancy's daughter, who was dressed as a fairy princess.

Maybe he had a point. I'd always butted heads with Nancy, but was it time to genuinely try to forge a more amicable relationship with her?

I looked over at Nancy, who caught my gaze. She stabbed a finger in Mikey's direction and glared at me. "Get him!" she mouthed.

While Adam and I were talking, I'd taken my attention off of Mikey and now he was splashing water at one of his friends. Still, he wasn't the only one doing it and she didn't have to be so mean. Although Adam may have made friends with her, there was no way I was ever going to do the same.

Desi arrived soon after and I pulled her aside to tell her about Adam and Nancy's new friendship.

"Seriously?" She wrinkled her nose. "Maybe she's nicer to men?"

I shook my head. "Maybe."

She pointed to her watch. "I think it's our turn to man the bounce house."

She was right.

"Let me go remind Adam that he's in charge of Mikey when he's not in the bounce house." I found Adam and told him.

Desi and I watched our boys playing in the bounce house for the next hour. When the carnival was winding down and they were the only kids left in the bounce house, I put Ella down on the inflatable, just beyond the door, and warned the boys not to bump her. She froze, not sure what was going on. They knelt down a foot or so away from her and gently bounced, causing her to float up and down. She grinned and scrambled away, further into the bounce house.

"Uh," I said to Desi. "Should I get her?"

She laughed. "She's fine. The boys will be careful."

Nancy came over to us. "No children under one in the bounce house. She's not one yet, is she?" She squinted at me.

"She'll be one in a few days."

"But she's not yet," she said firmly. "Get her out now. And close it down. We've got to get it put away."

I sighed. "Boys, can you please bring Ella out? It's time to go."

"Mommy! I want to stay longer."

"Sorry, buds," Desi said, sticking her head inside. "Time to go."

They reluctantly guided Ella over to the edge and followed her out of the bounce house. Adam, the kids, and I walked home, tired, but contented. Ella fell asleep in the stroller before we left the preschool parking lot and even all of the candy Mikey had consumed that evening wasn't enough to keep him awake. Adam ended up carrying him home the last two blocks.

"That was fun," Adam said, after we'd put the kids to bed.

I smiled. "It was." It was nice having him home. The last two years, I'd taken Mikey to the carnival myself. His new job might not provide much financial security yet and I was having a hard time adjusting to him constantly being underfoot, but we were already reaping the benefits of having him home.

15

The next day, I went with Desi to Lindstrom's department store at the mall to meet with Mindy's daughter. With all of the fruitless searching we'd done recently, I really hoped she'd have the key with her and that we would be able to locate the file Desi needed to do her treasurer job.

"What department does she work in?" The store was massive, with two floors and dozens of different departments. A singsong voice sounded over the loudspeaker, asking Mary to call extension 121. Perfume drifted over to us from the cosmetics area, making me sneeze. Usually, I tried to avoid walking past the perfume sprayers, but I wasn't sure where we were going in the store.

"She said Women's Dresses." Desi crossed the tile floor to check out a directory stationed at the bottom of the escalator. "Looks like it's on the second floor."

We rode the escalator to the second floor, enjoying the live piano music floating up through the atrium. At the top, bright skylights illuminated the shiny white and blue tiles.

All around us was women's clothing. How were we going to find Stacey's department?

A discreet sign hanging on one wall read "Women's Dresses."

"There." I pointed at it.

"Good eye," Desi said. She moved with purpose toward that area, stopping at the cash register.

One person was ahead of us in line, trying to negotiate with the clerk on the most complicated return ever. When it was finally our turn, Desi asked the clerk, "Do you know where I can find Stacey Stevens?"

"She's sorting dresses over there." The petite woman stood on her tiptoes and pointed toward a tall rack in the corner of the store.

Desi flashed her a grin. "Thanks!"

We walked over to the metal rack, which was thick with dresses, not seeing Stacey until we were practically on top of her. When we found her, she was holding a dress in the air and checking the tag.

"Can I help you?" Stacey asked, without looking away from her task of sorting the dresses by size.

"Hi, Stacey." Desi waited patiently for her to finally notice who we were.

"Oh, hi." She looked between us. "I remember seeing you both at the funeral. You came for the key, right? I wasn't sure you would." She turned her wrist over and checked the time. "The key is in my locker. I have a break in ten minutes, so I can get it then. Do you mind hanging out until then?"

"No problem," Desi said breezily. "I'm sure we can find something to do."

She ushered me away, into the forest of fancy dresses. "How about this dress for you? You'd look fabulous in it."

She held up a forest green silk ensemble with sequins around the neckline.

It was pretty, although I had nowhere to wear it. Still it was fun to play the dress-up game. I reached for it and flipped over the price tag. Six hundred dollars. Yikes.

"Put it back," I said, dropping the tag like it had burned me. "I can't afford that."

"You could try it on," she sang out.

"Uh huh." I shook my head. "I don't want to accidentally snag it and get stuck buying it."

"Fine," Desi pouted. She replaced it on the rod and rummaged through the other dresses on the racks. "How about this one for me?" She waggled her eyebrows.

I had to laugh. The dress was hot pink, with a flirty skirt and low neckline—perfect for a sixteen-year-old's prom, but the antithesis of something Desi would wear. "Oh, yes, that's definitely your style. I can totally see you wearing it to the next policeman's ball."

She held it against herself and swayed a little. "Wouldn't it make a good impression on Tomàs's co-workers?" She giggled and put it back. "Seriously, though, we need to get out on the town more. Have a reason to wear a nice dress. I feel like all I ever do anymore is change diapers and work. I need some fun."

"I think Everton has a mom prom every spring. Want to be my date?" I asked. I ran my fingers over a beautiful midnight blue satin dress that probably cost more than a week's salary. Desi had a point—we did need to do more things without the kids.

"Sounds fun. Let me know if you find out anything more about it." She continued looking through the dresses, this time with a more serious expression on her face.

"Hey," Stacey said as she approached us. "I'm going on break now. I'll be right out with the key."

"Great, thanks so much," Desi said. "I really appreciate how helpful you've been. When your mother's husband told us most of her belongings had already been placed in storage, I thought I'd never find it."

Stacey rolled her eyes. "Joseph. Ugh. I hate that guy. I was never so happy as when my mom told me she was divorcing him for some new guy." She shook her head. "She'd be turning over in her grave if she knew he got her life insurance policy."

Desi and I looked at each other.

"When we were at the apartment, he was in the middle of discussions with the insurance company," Desi said. "I was surprised that he'd inherited the money because I'd heard your mother was getting a divorce."

"I have no clue what happened," Stacey said. "She told me she'd changed the primary beneficiary back to me. I can't believe that loser will get two million dollars." She swore under her breath, then looked around, as if to make sure none of her co-workers had heard. "I know she wanted me to have it if she died."

"I'm so sorry," I said. "It's awful when the beneficiary on a life insurance policy isn't changed when relationships change. I had that happen to a friend of mine."

"Mom was always so careful about updating things. It seems strange she wouldn't have changed this. I'm going to challenge it, of course." She checked her watch again. "Anyway, I'd better get you the key before my break is over." She turned abruptly and made a beeline for a door near the other corner of the store.

We moved away from the dresses and slowly walked in the direction Stacey had gone. A few minutes later, she came out, holding a round orange keychain with one small key attached.

"Here." She handed it to Desi. "It's the Storage Lot in Everton, number 115."

"115," Desi repeated, rubbing her finger over the lettering on the front of the keychain. "Thanks. Do you want me to bring it back to you here?"

"Sure. I'm working until nine," she said. "Hey, if you find anything that might help me convince the insurance company that the money should be mine instead of Joseph's let me know." She pouted. "He doesn't even need the money. I'm the one with the big student loans to pay off."

"We will," I promised.

Desi nodded. "Thanks."

She disappeared back into the employee area. Desi and I rode the escalator downstairs and exited the building.

"That was kind of fun," Desi said. "We should go shopping more often. Have a girl's day."

"That MUMs fashion show really got to you, didn't it?" I grinned at her. She was right though, it had been fun.

"I did want to buy that matching mother–daughter outfit that Lina and I wore in the fashion show," Desi admitted. "But then I realized it would only fit her for a few months and then it would just be a mother outfit. It didn't seem so cute then."

"Next time maybe."

She beeped her minivan open and we got back into it.

"Do you have time to go to the storage unit with me?" Desi asked.

"I wouldn't miss it." I'd come this far, I might as well finish the quest. Plus, the day out with Desi had already been fun. Maybe we'd uncover buried treasure at the storage place.

16

"I swear she said Unit 151," Desi said. "I don't know why this isn't working." She stabbed the key into the lock another time.

I brushed my hair back with my hand and pulled my coat tighter against my torso. It was colder inside the multistory storageplex than it was outside.

"It's not working. Are you sure that's the right unit number? You've tried the lock a million times already. Why didn't you write down the unit number?" I asked.

"I was too caught up in thinking about Mindy's life insurance policy." She stared at the key. "It's not like you wrote it down either."

"True. But she handed you the key." I glanced down the hallway we'd come from. "Let's go back to the office. Maybe they'll give us the storage unit number."

"Fine." She pushed herself up from the ground.

We walked straight down the hall, stopping when we came to a fork in the path.

"Which way did we come from?" Both halls had glaring

fluorescent lighting and concrete floors that seemed to stretch forever.

She put her hands on her hips and alternated her gaze between the choices. "I'm pretty sure we came from that side." She jutted her chin out to the path to the right.

I shrugged. Her guess was as good as any, although I was beginning to feel as though we were locked in a corn maze that we couldn't get out of. "Maybe we'll find someone that we can ask for directions."

We turned down the path and walked about twenty feet.

"It smells like popcorn in here." Desi sniffed the air.

"You're right. But where's it coming from?" I paused and cocked my head to the side to listen. "I think I hear someone. Maybe they can tell us if we're going the correct way."

We followed the noise to a storage unit with the metal door rolled up about a foot off of the ground. A man's voice came from inside.

"Should we ask him?" Desi stared at the open storage unit. "It feels weird to shout out a question from under the door."

"I don't want to be wandering around here forever."

"Me neither." She shivered. "I'm starting to feel claustrophobic."

Desi had horrible claustrophobia and when it took full effect, she'd start reciting names of baked goods to calm herself down. I didn't want a full Desi meltdown in the middle of the hallway, so I crouched on the floor and looked under the door. *Whoa.*

"Did you see anyone?" she asked.

I yanked on her arm. "Yes. Let's go."

She allowed herself to be dragged down the hall, but I could tell she was itching to ask me about what I'd seen.

"What did you see in there?" she asked when were far

enough down the hall to not be heard by anyone in that unit.

"It was weird."

"What do you mean?" She narrowed her eyes at me. "Like there was a chop shop in there or something?"

I sighed. "There was a man sitting in his underwear in a recliner chair eating popcorn out of a bowl on his lap. He was watching football or something. There were pictures on the wall and a rug and everything—just like a house. So weird."

Desi laughed. "You found someone's man cave!"

"That's a thing?" I asked.

"Yep. Men rent out storage units and use them as their own private domains."

"Still, it's weird."

"Oh, yeah, I couldn't agree more." She pointed down the hall. "Hey, isn't that the office?"

Happily, she was right. We opened the office door, revealing a pimply-faced teenage boy behind the counter.

"Hi," Desi said brightly. "We need to get something out of a friend's storage unit and we can't remember the unit number. See, we have the key." She held it up in the air, the swinging silver key catching the light from above.

"What's your friend's name?" the boy asked, barely looking up.

"Stacey Stevens. It might still be under her mom's name, Mindy Danvers."

He turned and tapped the information into the computer. "Mindy Danvers, unit 115."

Relief washed over Desi's face. "No wonder I couldn't get the key to work. I thought it was unit 151."

"Uh huh." He went back to whatever he was doing. He

obviously couldn't care less if we got in the storage unit or not.

The office door slammed shut behind us and we walked back down the hallway, following the unit numbers this time to keep from getting lost. As we neared the man cave, a loud cheer erupted from it. Desi and I covered our mouths to smother laughter and hurried past it. When we reached unit 115, she inserted the key and, this time, it turned easily. She unclipped the lock and rolled up the metal door.

After she flipped on the light switch, I had to take a step back. The unit was piled high to the ceiling with boxes and furniture. A narrow pathway provided access to Mindy's belongings.

"This is going to take forever," I said.

"I think it will be fine. Be positive." Desi marched over to a cardboard box and poked it with her finger. "See, it's nicely labeled. Kitchen stuff."

Sure enough, someone had done a wonderful job of organizing the boxes and labeling them with a Sharpie. Idly, I wondered whether it had been Mindy's husband or daughter. It didn't really matter, but considering that Joseph and maybe even Stacey were suspects in my mind, it would have provided a little more insight into their character.

"Ok, so we just need to find the office boxes." I scanned the room. "I think there's some over there." I climbed over a couch and stood on a chair to reach a box at the top of a stack. Before pulling it down, I tested the weight, then carefully removed it, setting it on top of another chair.

"Maybe we'll be lucky and it'll be in the first box we try." Desi smiled.

I opened the box. Someone had written "Office" on it, but it appeared to only hold photos.

"She must have been really into taking pictures." Desi

lifted a stack of them. "Look here's one of her and Stacey on a boat at some lake."

I looked at the photo. Mindy and Stacey were smiling at the camera, having a carefree day out in the sun. They could have been any other mother and daughter on vacation together.

"She doesn't look like someone who would kill her mother." I rubbed my finger along the edge of the photo.

"Do you think she did it?" Desi asked.

"I don't know. I mean, she did say she thought she was the beneficiary of Mindy's life insurance policy, right?"

Desi nodded slowly. "Right. But that's a stretch. She could have just told us about that because she was mad about Joseph inheriting it instead."

"I suppose you're right." I glanced around. "We'd better get moving on this. I told Adam I'd be back by four to start dinner. After the Great Kitchen Rearranging, it's taking me twice as long to make dinner because I can't find anything in the kitchen."

She laughed. "You haven't put everything back yet where it goes?"

I grimaced. "No. I don't want to offend him, but it's driving me nuts."

"Well, let's get moving so you can get home." She replaced the photos in the cardboard box and folded the top closed. "Can you reach that other box?" She pointed at one next to the one I'd taken down.

"I think so."

This time, we had better luck. It was full of file folders and notebooks.

"Bingo," Desi said. "I bet it's in here."

I took out some of the folders and looked through them. "Not in these."

"Not these either." She picked up one of the last file folders in the box and opened it. Her eyes widened at the contents.

"Oh my gosh. You're never going to believe this."

"What?" I put the files I had just gone through back into the box and removed the last set, then leaned over to see what she had.

"Mindy wasn't so sweet after all." She plucked a sheet of paper covered in numbers. Someone had circled several of the figures with a black Sharpie. "I think this is a copy of the main ledger."

I looked up at her sharply. "The ledger you're looking for?"

"No, the main ledger for the district, not for our group."

Desi rifled through the folder. "She's got dirt on a ton of people. Every single paper in here is a note about a different person and their transgressions. This folder is like her little black book." She pulled the ledger copy away from the other papers. "This one doesn't have anyone's name on it, but if these are the books from this area's MUMs district, it appears she's questioning some of the transactions."

"How much money could the district office of MUMs possibly have running through it?" I asked. It seemed odd that a nonprofit organization like MUMs could have that much money in their coffers.

"You'd be surprised," Desi said. "They do lots of fundraisers like the haunted house and there's income from dues and classes too. Multiply that by all of the MUMs groups west of the Mississippi. I wouldn't be surprised if there was a couple hundred thousand in their bank account."

"You're kidding." I grabbed it from her and scanned the page. Desi was right—this did look like Mindy had been suspicious of someone. "Didn't Angela's husband say something about Mindy accusing her of stealing? She did have that forty grand just laying around in her office."

"And if Mindy told Angela she knew, Angela may have murdered her to keep her quiet. Maybe the police arrested the right person after all." Desi set the paper aside and took out another sheet of paper.

"Enter suspect number two. Apparently she had some dirt on Lisa too."

"What could she possibly have on Lisa?" I asked.

"You know those fancy hats and dolls she crochets and sells for hundreds of dollars each?"

"Yeah. So?"

"So they're homemade, but not by her. According to this account, she buys them from a Mexican woman and sells them as her own up here. Mindy caught Lisa at the post office receiving a shipment from Mexico."

"Technically, that's not illegal. They are handmade, so she's not advertising them fraudulently."

"Yeah, but the legality of her business isn't what's most important to Lisa. If her friends and customers found out she was a fraud, that would mean the end of a successful business for her."

"What else is there? Anyone else we know?" I tried to see the folder over Desi's shoulder.

"Not much else, but there's a photo of Drew in here. Looks like it was one of him and Angela, but Mindy cut Angela out of the photo. I wonder what she had on him? Except for the copy of the ledger, all of the others contained both the person's name and what she had over them."

"She did tell him about Angela's alleged embezzlement. Maybe she was blackmailing him to keep quiet?"

"Hmm. From what we've seen at her apartment and in

here, Mindy led a pretty quiet lifestyle. I don't remember seeing anything particularly high value. If she was profiting from these tidbits she knew, it wasn't showing up in her daily life. Where's the money?"

"I don't know." I leaned against a stack of boxes to think for a moment. "So Mindy knew a lot of people's big secrets, may have been a blackmailer, had an angry ex-husband and a money hungry daughter. It could have been anyone that killed her."

Desi nodded. "I think we need to talk to Lisa and find out if Mindy ever followed through on what she knew about her. I wish we could have found that ledger though. We're out of time for today and I don't want to borrow the key from Stacey again."

I picked up the files that I'd removed from the bottom of the box and rifled through them.

"Voila!" I held a green folder containing a ledger to Desi.

She glanced at it then held it to her chest. "I thought we'd never find this thing." She glanced around. "Now, let's get out of here. This place is creepy."

"I agree."

We put everything but the group's ledger back where we'd found it, including the incriminating information about Lisa and Angela, but not before snapping photos of them with Desi's phone camera—just in case.

Desi rolled down the storage unit's door and snapped the lock on it shut. We dropped off the key with Stacey at Lindstrom's, but neither of said anything to her about what we'd found.

When we were back in Desi's minivan, I turned to her and asked, "Why didn't you say anything to her about the folder with all of the blackmail-worthy information in it."

She shrugged. "If it were my mom, I wouldn't want to

know she'd kept such a thing. Stacey's mom was murdered
—right now, she doesn't need to know this about her on top
of everything else she's going through."

I nodded. Desi was right.

"I do want to ask Lisa about the crocheting though." I
thought about Desi fighting with the lock and remembered
finding Lisa standing in front of the storage shed by herself
the day of Mindy's murder. "She was the first person at
Angela's house that day."

"I know," Desi said grimly. "I hope she didn't have
anything to do with Mindy's death. But we should ask her
about what Mindy had on her. I don't want to be stuck on
thinking she's the murderer without having all the facts.
Maybe she never even knew that Mindy knew."

"I guess." I had my doubts about that. If Mindy had
accused Angela of embezzlement in front of her husband,
who knew what else she was capable of?

17

I would have liked to put off talking to Lisa about the crocheted hats, but Desi and I had both signed up for the baby and child CPR class that MUMs offered the next day.

"Where is everyone?" Desi asked. The parking lot outside the elementary school where the class would be held was empty.

I shrugged. "I don't know. I swear it said to meet at four o'clock." I checked my watch. "We're a couple of minutes early and Lisa did say none of the MUMs are ever on time, so maybe the others haven't arrived yet."

The doors were unlocked and, in a minute, we found ourselves standing outside the classroom. No one else was inside except Lisa. She saw us through the window in the door and waved at us. Reluctantly, we entered.

"Hey, girls," Lisa said, beaming at us. "I'm so happy to see you. But why are you here so early? I'm just getting things set up and the CPR instructor won't be here for another hour." She held out a sheaf of neatly stapled documents. "These are the instructions for Baby and Child CPR that I printed out for everyone."

Desi and I looked at each other.

"I thought you said four," Desi hissed at me under her breath.

"Maybe it was five?" I whispered back. I'd forgotten to write it down when Lisa had told us about the class the week before, but after the hard time I'd given Desi about not writing down the storage unit number, I hadn't wanted to admit to her that I didn't know for sure.

"We were excited to take this class," I said to Lisa. "I've always meant to attend one, but then life got in the way."

"It's so important though, isn't it?" Lisa said earnestly. "I feel every parent should go through it."

I nodded. My heart beat a little faster. This seemed like the perfect opportunity to talk with Lisa, but how were Desi and I going to bring up the Mexican crochet artist? It wasn't really something that came up naturally in conversation and I didn't want to just blurt it out.

Desi, on the other hand, had no such compunctions.

"While I was searching for the MUMs financial documents, we uncovered some unsettling information about your crocheting business."

"Oh, really? What?" Lisa stopped separating out the packets onto each desk in the classroom we were in and focused her attention on us.

"Mindy left a note stating that she'd seen you at the post office receiving a package from Mexico and you were telling the agent that it had crocheted hats in it. She said that someone else was creating the items that you sell as your own."

All the color drained out of Lisa's face. "What?"

Her legs wobbled and I helped her into a chair.

"She told me she wouldn't tell anyone," she whispered.

"So you did know," Desi said.

"Was Mindy blackmailing you?" I asked.

She shook her head. "No. Not now at least. She told me she knew what I was doing, but she hadn't made any threats to me. I always wondered when she'd use the information against me."

"Then why did she tell you she knew?" Desi asked.

"I don't know." She grimaced. "Mindy may have seemed nice, but she had a nasty streak running through her. You just never knew when it was coming out." She leaned forward toward the desk and her long blonde hair draped around her face. When she sat up, tears dripped down her cheeks. "You're not going to say anything to anyone are you?"

"I promise I won't say anything to the other MUMs, but I might need to tell the police about this." Desi kept her attention on Lisa's face.

"You don't think I killed Mindy, do you?" Lisa asked.

I couldn't make eye contact with her.

"I just need to make sure the police have all the information possible so they can solve this case," Desi said smoothly.

"Ok." Lisa dried her tears on her sleeve. "Hey, why are you two involved in the murder investigation anyway?"

"Well, we were all there when Mindy's body was found and we promised to tell the police if we noticed anything that seemed suspicious," I said.

"Oh. They didn't say anything like that to me." She sniffed again.

"It's probably because Desi's husband is a local cop." Desi glared at me, but I ignored her. "Did you make any of those hats yourself?"

Lisa nodded. "At first, I made all of them, but then the orders came in and I was such a success. I couldn't keep up with all of them and still be a good mom and keep my house clean. Something had to give, so when an acquaintance mentioned they'd seen similar items when they were on a vacation in Mexico, I decided to track down the crochet artist."

She dabbed her face again. "She's wonderful to work with and I can do all of the designs—really, I can. I just don't have the time for it. Everything is still handmade—just not by me."

"But still, if it got out, that wouldn't be good for you," I said, handing her a tissue from my purse.

She accepted it and smiled at me gratefully before blowing her nose. "No. I'd probably lose at least 50 percent of my business. My husband's company has been unstable lately and we really count on the money from my business. I can't afford to lose it."

"Well, you don't have to worry. If anyone in the group finds out the truth, it won't be from us," Desi said firmly.

"Thank you both. I appreciate it." The color returned to her face and, in a brighter voice, she said, "Since you're here anyway, can you help me put these out on every desk? I want to make sure everything is ready for when the instructor gets here."

"Sure." Desi grabbed the stack of paper and handed me half. When we finished distributing them, we met in the back of the room.

"I'm thinking we should have confronted her after class." I looked over at Lisa, who was near the window, typing something into her phone. "Now we have to be around her for another two hours."

"I know. It's awkward. But I saw an opening and I went

for it." She shrugged. "At least now we know what happened —at least the way Lisa tells it."

"Do you think she's lying?" I whispered.

"I don't know. From what I've seen, Lisa's business is built around her reputation and the cache of her brand. If the other moms in the group and her other customers found out, her name would be dragged through the mud. Anyway, it's not my business to call her out on it. I'll tell Tomàs so he can let the investigators know that it could be a factor, but that's the extent of it."

I nodded. "I agree. We stay out of it."

"I did kind of want to get one of her unicorn hats for Lina though," Desi said. "Now I feel weird ordering one."

"It's still the same hat," I said.

"Yeah, but now it feels tainted—we don't know that she isn't the killer."

"True."

Before we could continue our conversation, other women entered the room, gabbing amongst themselves. We claimed desks near each other and became model students for the rest of the evening. I made sure to avoid eye contact with Lisa.

Desi and I were the first to leave the class, making sure to avoid Lisa. We reached Desi's car first. She opened the door and started to get in.

"Don't forget Ella's birthday party tomorrow."

She smiled. "Don't worry. I'm still bringing an Elmo cake."

"Thank you, Aunt Desi." I laughed. "Seriously though, the kids are going to grow up remembering all of the cool cakes you've made them for their birthdays throughout the years. My grandmother made all of our birthday cakes when I was a kid and I still remember them fondly."

"Of course," she said. "I really don't mind. I don't get to use my cake decorating skills as much as I'd like nowadays. I love that I get to bake almost every day for the Boathouse and the BeansTalk, but sometimes it gets a little old to make the same things over and over again. I've got to dust off some of my mom's old recipes and branch out a little."

"Maybe you could start selling them to that place in the mall," I teased.

"Maybe." Her tone was serious. "I've been thinking about what you said to me before about it. Once Lina's a bit older, I may give it a try. After having the BeansTalk threatened by Mr. Westen, it's made me realize how important it is to diversify my business."

I nodded. "I think you'd be good at it. Just think, you'll have the Torres baking and catering empire soon."

"Yeah, maybe not soon, but someday." She gave me a goofy smile. "I'll see you tomorrow night."

"See you." I walked over to my car. I was a little surprised by Desi's change of mind about baking for the coffee stand, but I shouldn't have been. She was always up for a challenge and even motherhood hadn't slowed her down.

I could also understand why Lisa hadn't turned down the extra business once her crochet creations had taken off. It would be hard to stare at success and give it up so easily, especially when the income was needed. Still, it did give her even more of a motive to kill the person who was threatening her livelihood.

———

18

I'd planned a low-key first birthday party for Ella, only inviting our family over for dinner and cake. My parents planned to drive in from Idaho. They hadn't been to visit us since August, so I was happy to have the chance to see them. Like last time they'd come to visit, they'd insisted on staying in a hotel.

Normally, I'd protest that, but this time, I was grateful. Our house was a mess and I didn't know if I could mentally deal with having both of my parents at our house for an extended period of time, knowing they weren't together anymore.

Of course, I'd left most of the preparation for the afternoon of the party. I was rushing around the kitchen, cooking enough lasagna to feed an army, when Adam came in.

"I hung up all of those Elmo decorations we had left over from Mikey's party a few years ago."

I nodded quickly. "Great. I can't wait to see her reaction when she sees Elmo." I smiled, thinking about how she loved to dance holding on to her little table while Elmo sang on TV. My baby was growing up. It was a little sad, but I was excited to see her personality developing.

"You ok in here?" Adam asked, raising an eyebrow. "We're having our parents and my sister's family over, not the entire town."

"I know. I hate to be short on food." Looking around the kitchen though, I realized I may have overdone it. Oh well, there'd be plenty of lasagna to freeze for quick meals during the long winter.

"When are they coming again?" he asked.

"I invited everyone for six. My parents called a few hours ago to let me know they were in Ericksville, so we should be able to start dinner on time."

"Sounds good. I'll finish setting up the table." He came over and kissed my forehead. "It's going to be a great party."

I readied the salad to toss with dressing right before serving and popped the garlic bread in the oven. Desi had brought over the Elmo cake along with a smaller smash cake that I'd set on the counter. Everything looked great. Sweat dripped down my back and I pulled the ratty T-shirt I'd worn for cooking and cleaning away from my body.

"I'm going upstairs to take a quick shower," I called to Adam. We'd dropped the kids off with Lincoln that afternoon so we'd be free to prep for the party. Having them gone had made the difference between two and six hours of prep time.

While I was drying my hair, I heard an ominous crash in the kitchen. I rushed out of the bathroom and shouted down the stairs.

"What was that?"

"Uh, I don't want you to freak out," Adam called back up.

I immediately ran down the stairs, coming to a sliding halt at the entrance to the kitchen. Adam stood there, dragging Goldie away from a pan of lasagna that had fallen to the floor.

"I thought he was locked up in the family room." I eyed Adam.

"He must have escaped when I got the vacuum out. That door doesn't always close all the way," Adam said sheepishly. "Sorry, honey."

I shut my eyes for a moment then reopened them. Yep, half the lasagna I'd made was splattered all over the kitchen floor and cabinets. There was probably enough food left to feed everyone, but it was going to take a while to clean it all. I had half a mind to allow Goldie to take on the job, but decided that I didn't need a sick dog added to the mix.

"I'm going to go upstairs to get dressed. I can help you clean it when I get back, ok? Please lock Goldie back up so he doesn't eat it all."

Goldie whined and strained against Adam's grip on his collar.

"Sorry, buddy," Adam said. "But you got both of us in trouble. Back to the family room you go."

Goldie trotted along beside Adam as he led him back to doggy jail.

When I got back downstairs, my hair dried and dressed in clothes more appropriate for a birthday party, the floor was almost clean.

"Whoa. How'd you get it cleaned so fast?" I asked. Adam was on the floor washing off the bottom cupboards.

"He had some help," came a male voice from the hallway leading to the garage.

My mom and dad popped out of the hallway, enveloping me in a big group hug.

"Hi, honey," my mom said, squeezing me tight. "You look stressed."

"Thanks, Mom." I sighed. "I'll be fine after Halloween."

She waggled her finger at me. "Exercise will keep the stress away, remember that."

"I know." I smiled to myself. Once a P.E. teacher, always a P.E. teacher. "Hey, Dad." I gave him a hug too. "It's so great to see you both."

They exchanged glances. I looked from one of them to the other.

"What? Am I missing something?"

My mother leaned forward to kiss my dad on the lips and he wrapped his arm around her waist. They both grinned at me. My eyes widened.

"You're back together?" Part of me didn't dare believe it. They'd been separated for almost half a year and the longer it had been, the more I'd lost hope of them ever reuniting.

"After spending five months in the basement, I realized that I couldn't live without this woman." My dad pulled her tighter to him and she blushed.

Adam came in and wrapped his arm around my waist. "Good news, huh?"

That was the understatement of the year. "Yeah." I could barely speak, but joy welled up inside of me with the force of Old Faithful.

My mother broke away from my dad and clapped her hands. "No more time for lollygagging—we've got to get this house ready for a party."

I smiled and went over to my list. Almost everything on it was already done.

"Adam, would you do me a favor and grab that straight-back chair out of your office? We're one short."

"On it," he answered.

"Mom, can you please set the table?" I asked. Adam had

already installed the extra leaves in our table, making it long enough for everyone to have a place to sit.

"Sure, honey." She reached up into the cupboard and pulled down some plates and cups, then searched in the bottom cupboard. "Hey, Jill, where are Mikey's cups? I swear they used to be in here."

I sighed. "They were. Adam did some rearranging."

"Oh," my mother said knowingly. "I'm sure it was very *helpful* too."

"Yeah. He's been very *helpful*, lately." We looked at each other and laughed.

She held her hand up to shield her mouth and whispered, "I'll have to tell you about all the *helpful* things your dad has done since he retired."

I pinched my lips together to try to keep from smiling and turned to my dad, who was standing at the edge of the kitchen looking confused by the conversation between Mom and me. "Can you please light a fire? It's getting a bit chilly in here."

He nodded and strode over to the wood fireplace. My mother carried out a stack of plates.

Adam came back with the extra chair and entered the kitchen, coming up behind me. "I'm so happy for you, honey," he whispered into my ear.

Tears dripped down my cheeks and I turned my head to the side before I wiped them away. "Me too."

The doorbell rang, and I opened it to find Desi's family and my in-laws on the porch. Lincoln held a mountain of presents. Anthony and Mikey ran into the house and made a beeline for the stairs.

"Ella's one—I don't think she needs that many gifts," I teased.

"Beth went a little crazy at the toy store," he said. His wife elbowed him.

"I did not. There are clothes in there too," she said defensively.

"Hey, some of us would like to get inside. It's pouring buckets out here," Desi said, brushing past them, with Lina clutched to her chest. She removed her muddy shoes and placed them on the mat by the door and hung her dripping coat up on the coat rack. Then, she plopped herself down on the couch and my mom sat next to her, cooing over Lina. On the love seat, my father held Ella, bouncing her on his knee and singing a song he'd sung to me as a child. With the fire going and the rain pattering on the porch roof outside while my family communed, I felt warm, safe, and happy.

Mikey and Anthony bounded down the stairs, playing a game involving vinyl dinosaurs and lots of growling. I grinned. Tomàs was filling glasses with milk and water while Adam and I carried the food to the table.

"Dinner's ready!" I called out. My family came to the table, sitting down together to celebrate my daughter's birthday.

After we'd all eaten a helping, my mother put down her fork and asked, "Is everything on track for the haunted house? I'm looking forward to seeing it."

Adam nodded. "I think so. Most of the construction will be done by tomorrow."

I sighed with relief. I'd tried to stay out of the day-to-day logistics of the haunted house and to not step on Adam's toes, but I'd been dying to know how things were going. Luckily, my mom had asked for me.

"That's great that you and Jill have the opportunity to work together. John and I always enjoyed teaching at the same school," my mother said approvingly.

Dad laughed. "Well, not always. Ann always wanted me to chaperone the school dances with her and I couldn't say no because she'd already volunteered me to the rest of the staff."

She shrugged and laughed too. "I didn't want to get stuck there by myself."

Tomàs cleared his throat. "So, we had something strange happen down at the station today."

Desi looked up at him. "What happened?"

"A woman came in asking for me in regard to the Mindy Danvers case." He eyed Desi and she squirmed. "You wouldn't know anything about that, would you?"

"Uh." Her eyes met mine. "I don't know?"

My heart hammered. Angela was already in police custody. Was it Lisa? Or Stacey? Would whoever it was have said anything to Tomàs about Desi and me asking questions? Tomàs had warned us in the past to stay out of active police investigations and we did our best to comply, but sometimes things just came up while we were doing everyday activities. At least that's what I told myself.

"Her name was Lisa Aldane. Ring a bell?"

"She's the leader of our MUMs group," Desi said.

I nodded. "What did she say?" Had Lisa confessed?

"Apparently she'd talked to you two and decided she needed to come clean about the origins of the hats she makes." He shook his head. "She seemed really worked up about it, but I don't think it has anything to do with the investigation."

"So did she confess?" Desi leaned forward, her eyes big.

I held my breath. It would be nice if this was all over.

He gave us a strange look. "No. All she said was she wanted us to know about her crocheted hat business." His eyes narrowed in on Desi. "You wouldn't know anything about why she felt the sudden need to confess something like that, would you?"

"Jill and I talked with her yesterday at the CPR class we attended. When we were in Mindy's storage unit looking for the MUMs financial ledger, we came across some information about her business and we asked her about it. That's all."

The rest of our family had been quiet as they watched the exchange between Desi and Tomàs.

"You were in the dead woman's storage unit?" Adam asked. Mikey's head shot up, suddenly paying attention to the grown-ups.

Now it was my turn to squirm. "Well, the ledger wasn't at her apartment."

Tomàs's eyes bulged so much that I thought they were going to fall out of his head. "Her apartment. You were in her apartment? Seriously?"

"It was official MUMs business. We didn't go there to snoop," Desi said.

He gave her a long look. "Ok, but try to stay out of the investigation. Someone killed that woman and I don't want you involved with it."

She nodded, but the festive mood had dissipated.

Adam rapped on his glass with the tines of his fork. "Is anyone ready to open presents?"

Anthony and Mikey cheered, even though the presents weren't for them.

We cleaned up the table and gathered around the fireplace. I sat on the floor with Ella as Mikey scooted presents over to her to rip open. Anthony hovered anxiously over his cousins. When Ella struggled to open them, they were eager to help. Soon, she had a pile of open gifts next to her. Unsurprisingly, the boys became infatuated with a ball-spitting elephant toddler toy.

Adam checked his watch. "We'd better have cake soon if we want to get the kids into bed at a decent hour."

Sure enough, it was almost eight, half an hour past Mikey's bedtime.

"Time for cake!" I shouted as I walked into the kitchen to retrieve it.

I set it on the dining room table as everyone gathered around. Adam lit the first birthday candle and we sang happy birthday to Ella. The boys gave her a little help with the candle, but then she grabbed the small chocolate Elmo cake in front of her and smashed it into her mouth. Red icing covered her face as she shoveled more and more cake in.

"Well, I think she takes after her mother," Adam quipped.

I glared at him and he grinned back at me. Goldie had escaped from the family room, probably let out by the boys, and he hoovered around on the floor for crumbs. I guided him out and led him back to doggy jail.

"Sorry. Chocolate isn't good for dogs." On the way back, I saw my whole family sitting there, enjoying Desi's wonderful baking, and I was overcome with how lucky I was to have all of them. Life wasn't always perfect, but I knew we were always there for each other.

Everyone retreated to the living room after the cake had been consumed, except Desi and me, who were cleaning up.

"I can't believe Lisa confessed to the police," Desi whispered as she ran a rag over the table top.

"Me neither." I stacked up the remaining dishes to take into the kitchen. "But doesn't that support her innocence? I mean, it's going to get out that she doesn't make all of the products she sells. If it was such a big secret that she would kill to protect it, I don't think she'd have done that."

"Probably not," Desi said. "But then who did it?"

"I don't know." I glanced at our family, chatting and laughing in the other room. "But if we're going to find out, we'd better do it on the down-low."

"No kidding. We promised all of them that we'd be careful. If something else comes up about our involvement, I think Tomàs is going to freak out."

"Agreed."

After Desi helped me clean up the table, she edged toward the door. "We'd better get going. I think Anthony's about to fall asleep standing up."

I glanced at Anthony, leaning on his dad, his eyes half-closed.

Laughing, I said, "Thanks for coming."

Desi put her coat on and the rest of them followed, including my parents. Tomàs helped Anthony put his shoes on and the adults did the awkward dancing at the front door routine as they all tried to put their shoes on at the same time.

"Sorry about the mess." Desi looked ruefully at the muddy outlines of their shoes on the hardwood floor next to the door. "Hopefully Mikey doesn't smear that all over the rugs."

Rain and dirt tracked into the house were all just part of the fun of living in the Pacific Northwest. At Angela's house, when I saw the mud oozing from Drew's shoes, I'd had the same worry as Desi—that I'd get it all over the spotless interior of Lincoln's truck. Luckily, I'd managed to return the truck to him in the same condition it was when I'd borrowed it, and I hoped I could keep Mikey away from this mess long enough to get the mop. That kid did like playing in the dirt.

"Don't even worry about it. I'll clean it up when you're gone." I smiled at her.

Everyone waved goodbye and they were gone. Our house felt suddenly empty with just Adam, me, and the kids. They'd helped me clean up so much that the muddy imprints of their shoes near the front door were one of the few reminders that we'd just had a party. All of the party energy had drained out of me and I yawned. Although some people had big parties for their child's first birthday, I was glad we'd had a more intimate gathering. Ella wouldn't remember much of it anyway and the pictures would remind her she'd been surrounded by everyone she loved.

19

"Seriously? You thought it was a good idea to put that in the corner? That was front and center in my design." Angela fumed in front of me as she took in the decorating that we'd done in her absence. Adam had made the grievous mistake of placing a particularly realistic zombie near the corner of the first room.

I bit my tongue, literally, forcing myself to calm down. Part of me wished the police had held Angela longer, but they hadn't had enough evidence to keep her locked up and now she was out, torturing me.

"You weren't here. We had to do something to get the haunted house ready. We open in only two days." In my opinion, the haunted house looked great. It was spooky now, with the bright overhead lights, and would be even more frightening in the dark.

"Well," she huffed, "if you and your sister-in-law hadn't discovered a body in my yard, this never would have happened."

I cocked my head to the side. Did she really say that?

Somehow Mindy's murder had become Desi's and my fault, although I was pretty sure neither of us had been responsible for killing her.

"Again, I tried to get your designs, but we couldn't find them at your house and Drew said he wasn't able to see you to get them." I leaned against the doorframe, watching her face grow redder by the minute.

She turned to face me, her eyes ablaze. "That idiot. My lawyer said that Drew refused to visit me in jail. Said he didn't want to see me that way. He couldn't even figure out how to pay for my bail, leaving me stuck there for this whole time." She huffed again. "Well, he can forget about seeing me ever again. Not that it's any of your business, but I intend to divorce that jerk as soon as I get this legal matter cleared up."

It amazed me how she brushed off being the police's prime suspect in a murder investigation. And although I never saw her and Drew getting along, I hadn't seen them together much. He'd seemed devoted to her when he asked Desi and me to investigate Mindy's murder and reluctant to tell us about the embezzlement that Mindy had accused her of.

We were interrupted by a delivery man rolling a tall box along on a dolly. "Where should I put this?"

I gave him a confused look. "What is it? I'm not expecting any deliveries today."

"That's mine," Angela said to me. "I saw what you'd done to my haunted house and I knew that I needed to do something to improve it, so I had this rushed over from a local prop store." She turned back to the man. "You can put it over there."

She pointed to one section of the haunted house and he unloaded it against the wall there. In my opinion, my husband had risen to the challenge of decorating the haunted house. He'd come up with creative scenarios on the spur of the moment—or at least I hoped they hadn't been lurking in his mind forever. Adam had managed to enlist the help of several of Lincoln's carpenter friends and built the farmhouse, plus a barn and graveyard nearby. What could Angela have possibly ordered to add?

I followed her over to the cardboard box. She ripped the sides open with a set of keys she pulled out of her oversized purse and spread it open. Packing peanuts spilled out all over the hardwood floors, revealing an Egyptian sarcophagus, the twin of the one where Mindy's body had been hidden.

I gasped, too many memories flashing back into my mind. Besides, what did Egypt have to do with a creepy haunted farm theme?

She gave me a satisfied look. "Now I can really get started on this."

I had to leave the room before I punched her in the face. It was my turn to fume. Adam had spent too many hours in the last week making this the best haunted house Ericksville had ever seen and now Angela wanted to undo his hard work?

It was if Angela had sucked all the oxygen out of the room. I walked outside to the parking lot to get some fresh air. The skies were gray, but thankfully, it wasn't raining. I circled the building until I was on the side by the lighthouse. For a few minutes, I focused my attention on the historic building and grounds, allowing the familiar sight to calm me. I liked to imagine what Ericksville must have looked like when it was operational. When I felt better, I turned around and walked back toward the front door of the

Boathouse. In the parking lot, Adam was just getting out of his car and I waited for him outside.

When he neared me, he said, "Whoa. You look mad enough to spit nails."

Perhaps my anger hadn't mellowed as much as I'd thought.

I gritted my teeth. "Come inside. You'll see."

Adam gave me a hug, then opened the door for us to enter. "What's wrong?"

I shook my head and grabbed his hand, dragging him over to the main room.

"What did you think of it?" he asked eagerly. "I only have a few last touches to do on it."

"I loved it," I said heatedly. "But she has other ideas." I poked my finger in Angela's direction, where she was easing the sarcophagus out of the box.

His gaze followed my finger. "What is she doing? Who is that?"

"That's Angela Laveaux." I pursed my lips. "And she thinks she's making the scenes better."

"Over my dead body," he said. "That's not happening." He strode over to her.

I hung back by the door, letting them hash it out before I got involved. This was Adam's baby and I wanted to let him talk to Angela first.

"Hey, I'm Adam," he said.

"Ok? So?"

"So I'm the one who took over the design of the haunted house after you were indisposed." He smiled at her. "My wife, Jill, mentioned you might have some feedback for me."

She snorted. "Feedback? This needs to get ripped out." To emphasize her point, she shoved a hay bale aside to make room for her sarcophagus.

He stepped back. "My crew and I have put a lot of work into this, and I'm happy with the results."

"Well, I'm in charge of the haunted house this year and I say this all needs to go." She swept her hands dramatically across the room.

"Don't you like the haunted farm theme?"

"No. It looks like something you found on Pinterest. So derivative."

Whoa. After watching Adam with Nancy, I'd begun to think he was a snake charmer in disguise, but it looked like this was one asp he couldn't control. He looked like he was about to say something, but I stepped in first.

"I'm sorry, Angela, but you need to leave."

Her mouth gaped open. "What did you say?"

"I said you need to leave." I smiled pleasantly at her, but my voice held a steely undertone. "We're hosting the event here at the Boathouse and I'm overruling you. Adam was nice enough to step in when you weren't here. I'm sorry about this, but you're going to need to wait until next year to implement your ideas." I spun her around and gently guided her toward the door. She sputtered the whole way there.

"You'll be sorry about this. I can make being in a local MUMs group miserable for you."

"Ah. Well, I'll have to risk that." I waved at her as she exited the door, locking it tightly behind her.

"I didn't think you had it in you," Adam said from behind me. "You're always so calm and polite to the Boathouse's clients, no matter how rude they are to you."

I shrugged. "She deserved it. No one talks to my husband like that. And she's not really the client—the Ericksville Chamber of Commerce is." I locked eyes with him. "Thank you for working so hard on this. I didn't know how we'd get it all done, but you've done an amazing job."

He blushed, making me laugh. Then he wrapped me in a huge hug.

"Thanks, honey."

"No problem." My voice was muffled by his chest.

Beth came out of her office. "I heard you arguing with Angela. Is everything all right?"

"It is now," Adam said.

"Angela wanted to make some last minute changes to the haunted house. And by last minute, I mean to change everything. She wasn't too polite in her demands or assessment of the current decorations either."

Beth's lips formed an O. "I thought it looked great."

"Me too," I agreed. "Which is why I told Angela she needed to get out of here." I looked up at her, suddenly anxious. While in the heat of the moment, it had felt good to tell Angela off, the Boathouse belonged to my in-laws. Angela might be a witch, but she had influence in town. "I hope you don't mind."

Beth laughed. "Nope. I would have told her off months ago, but you seemed to be able to handle her. I would have done the same thing if I'd heard her insult Adam's hard work." She smiled at her son. "Are you sure you don't want to join the Boathouse crew?"

He held up his hands. "I'm good, thanks. Actually, I have a lead on a new client at the office, so I'd better get over there."

She nodded.

"I'll see you back at the house tonight," he said to me, giving me a kiss on the cheek. "Bye, Mom." He gave Beth a quick hug.

I unlocked the doors for him to leave.

"Lunch?" Beth asked. "My treat."

I was relieved that she wasn't mad at me, but I knew I hadn't seen the last of Angela yet. Maybe lunch would alleviate the acid churning in my stomach.

I smiled at her. "Lunch sounds great. Thanks."

20

The Friday before Halloween finally arrived—opening night. My advertising efforts had paid off and a crowd was already starting to form outside the Boathouse, two hours before we officially opened. Lincoln had instructed the setup crew to create a waiting area in the parking lot with double stacked hay bales. Judging by how many people were already there, we'd need the overflow parking across the street tonight.

Creepy noises from the soundtrack Beth had ordered online floated through the air from a speaker set up near the door. For once, the weatherman had been right, and as day turned to dusk, we found ourselves enjoying a cool but clear night, complete with a full moon. Everything was shaping up to be a cackling good time.

To get into the spirit, all of the Boathouse staff and the MUMs members who were helping that night had dressed in clothes appropriate for working on a farm. Lisa had arrived, clothed in a pristine pair of overalls and a crisp gingham shirt. We'd put her to work chatting up the crowd.

Adam and I were both going to work the opening night, so our parents were going to take all of the kids out to a new indoor sports place in the area that had bouncy houses and arcade games. When my folks showed up, we ushered them in through a side door. I'm not sure how the crowd would have reacted if we'd allowed them in via the front door.

"Do we get to see the haunted house before we go?" my dad asked.

I nodded. Beth and Lincoln had already gone through, so they volunteered to watch the kids.

"I want to see it!" whined Mikey.

"Me too," said Anthony.

I knelt in front of Mikey. "Sorry, sweetie. The person who's running the kids' section of the haunted house isn't here yet. I'll take you through it tomorrow, ok?"

He sulked, but allowed his grandparents to take him and his cousin away to one of the other rooms, no doubt to bribe them with cookies or candy.

Adam and I stood with my parents at the entrance to the haunted house. It would be my first time through it in the dark and with the fog machines running.

"I'm a little nervous," Adam admitted.

I squeezed his hand. "Don't worry. It'll be great."

We let my parents go first, and while I said it was to be polite, in reality, I wanted to see their reactions. Although Halloween had never been huge in our household growing up, my mom was known for her love of horror movies, but they never failed to terrify her. Maybe that's why she liked them so much.

The overhead lights were off. The only visible light in this section was a fake full moon that Adam's crew had constructed, oddly similar to the real one outside. He'd used tall wooden sets to create a lonely road leading up to a farm, like something right out of a zombie movie or any other horror movie for that matter. A draft fluttered the corn stalks next to me and caused me to shiver.

"Brr," my mother said, wrapping her arms tight. She was so focused on the sudden chill that she didn't notice the undead approaching. Two realistic-looking zombies approached us, walking in a zigzag pattern, too close for comfort.

"Ahh!" she screamed.

Adam grinned and whispered to me, "I told them to get close to people. Looks like they're creepy enough."

We quickened our pace and the path turned before the zombies could reach us. We came out in the middle of a lonely graveyard, set in the middle of a cornfield. Some of the tombstones wiggled and fog oozed from the graves.

The farmhouse was the haunted house's finale. They'd created a terrifyingly realistic front porch with a door that creaked as you walked over the threshold. Inside, blood streaked the floor and fog seemed to come out of every crevice. I shivered again, right before a woman jumped out at us with a bloody knife.

"Ah!" This time it was my dad screaming. The woman with the knife didn't seem to notice us and just walked by, as though we were the ghosts. Further into the kitchen, we saw the woman's husband, lying dead on the floor. Ominous organ music came from behind a closed door.

By the time we'd exited the haunted house into the cool night air, all of us were laughing.

"I loved the murderous wife in the farmhouse," I said.

"Yeah, I figured you would." Adam laughed. "I'd better get out to the front to start taking people's money though. I think we'll be sold out tonight." He strode across the deck to the doorway back to the indoor areas.

"This was even better than what I imagined," my mother said. "Even your dad was scared." She smiled at him.

"I wasn't scared," he bluffed. "The woman with the knife startled me."

"Uh huh." She smiled knowingly and patted his hand. "Right." She turned to me. "What was up with the sarcophagus at the end though? It didn't seem to fit with the theme."

I rolled my eyes. "That's a long story."

She laughed.

"Thanks, you guys. I'm really glad you were able to see it," I said. "If you'd like you can go through again tomorrow with Mikey and see the kids' section. Adam outdid himself there, too, although it's much less frightening."

My dad nodded. "I'll go again." He looked at my mom and they communicated without speaking.

"Honey," my mom said, "we're a little worried that you've gotten yourself into another murder investigation."

"After hearing Tomàs mention it at Ella's birthday party, we asked Beth and Lincoln about what was going on. They told us that the woman who was supposed to design this haunted house has been arrested for the murder," Dad said. "That's a little too close to home for our comfort."

"That's true, she has been arrested," I said carefully.

"So the police are sure that this woman is the culprit?" My mother looked around the dock nervously, as if expecting someone to jump out at her even outside of the haunted house.

"Hmmm," I said. I didn't think it was a good idea to tell them that Angela was out on bail. Besides, I didn't really think that she had done it although I wasn't 100 percent certain. That also wasn't something I wanted to tell my parents, or they would've locked me up until I was sixty.

"We aren't trying to interfere with your life, honey," my father said. "It's just we are so far away usually and we want to make sure you're safe."

I wrapped an arm around his waist, giving him a squeeze. "I know. And I'll be careful, I promise."

"Well, we love you, and we don't want anything bad to happen to you," my father said in a gruff voice.

"We better get back inside, so we can meet up with Beth and Lincoln to take the kids to that arcade place. We'll bring the kids back to your house before bedtime and stay with them until you get home." My mother linked arms with my father. "You think you'll be home by eleven, right?"

I felt as though I were a kid agreeing to a curfew with my parents. "Yes, it ends officially at ten, so we should be done with cleanup by eleven."

My mom nodded. "See you later, honey. Have fun."

"Have fun with the kids."

They walked off, arm in arm. Despite the cool weather, warmth filled my heart. I knew it was unrealistic to expect that every marriage could be salvageable, but in my parents' case, there didn't seem to really be a big catalyst for their separation. That fact had always given me hope that they would one day return to being a couple.

I looked out over the water, where the full moon had risen high in the sky above Willoughby Island. It cast a cool glow into the inky depths of Puget Sound below. At this time of year and time of night, there were few boats out on the water except the ferry boat that crossed between Ericksville and Willoughby Island.

From behind me, shouts and screams floated through the air from the haunted house. Soon, the deck would be inundated by excited teenagers. I took one last look at the peacefulness of the water, and went back inside the Boathouse through the side entrance. So far, this had been a wonderful evening and I hoped that nothing would happen to change that.

21

*U*nfortunately, things don't always go according to plan. When I reentered the boathouse, I found Angela Laveaux sneaking around. I really wasn't in the mood to deal with her or her shenanigans.

"Angela, what are you doing here?" I asked. "The haunted house is ready to go—you can't make any changes to it."

"I know." A wistful expression crossed her face. "I'm not here to make any trouble, but I had to come. The haunted house has been mine ever since it started. Even if the design isn't mine this year, I still want—no, need, to be a part of it. Please, Jill. I know I behaved badly earlier, but I want to help. I don't have much else going for me now."

I didn't know what to think. The Angela I knew would never have admitted any weaknesses. I studied her silently. She was uncharacteristically subdued, whether from being a suspect in Mindy's murder or because of issues in her marriage. She looked like she was telling the truth, and I could understand where she was coming from. Unless she truly was the one who killed Mindy, she hadn't caused any of this to happen, and had merely been an innocent victim of the whole thing. I didn't want to take away the haunted house from her as well, although there wasn't much for her to do at this point. I racked my brain trying to come up with something that would make her feel useful.

"You know, I bet Adam could use some help out front, selling tickets. Would you be willing to do that?"

Her face lit up. "Oh, yes, that will be great. I love seeing how excited and scared people are before they go in." She looked down at her clothing. "But I don't have anything to wear." I assessed her attire. She wore a black corduroy jumper over a red and black plaid shirt. The corduroy didn't exactly fit in with our farmhouse theme, but I could work with that.

"Come with me," I said. I motioned in the direction of my office. "I brought in an extra pair of overalls, just in case someone needed a change of clothes or we got some extra volunteers. They should fit you."

"Thanks," she said, smiling at me gratefully.

I got Angela set up outside taking tickets with Adam and then I patrolled the Boathouse to make sure there weren't any stray guests wandering the rest of the grounds. When the last person went through for the night, we sent the MUMs and other volunteers home. Only Angela, Adam, Desi, and I remained. The cleaning crew would come through in the morning, but for now, I wanted to get everything straightened up and ready for the next night's haunted house.

"Desi, can you help me make sure we've got enough snacks for tomorrow? If not, we'll need to make some in the morning." We'd sold a lot of cupcakes and other goodies to people who'd gone through the haunted house and I wasn't sure we had enough left. It was already ten thirty, and I was crossing my fingers that I wouldn't have to come in early to help Desi with the baking.

"Sure." She set down the prop she was moving back into place.

Angela and Adam were hanging up the cast costumes and organizing the makeup tables so everything would be ready to go for the next day. The volunteers dressed as zombies had cast off their clothing in a heap in the makeshift dressing room and the stage makeup was in shambles. Angela seemed happy to be a part of the team and hadn't made a peep about any of the decorations or how we were running things.

"If these weren't volunteers, I wouldn't be very happy," Adam said, eying the mess. He handed me the master remote for the fog machine. "I have no idea how this got here, but can you please return it to the entrance for me when you go?"

I nodded and took it from him. "They may be messy, but we're lucky the volunteers stayed until the end."

Desi and I left to determine our supply levels. Luckily, it appeared that we were good for another day. There was plenty of popcorn, apples for dipping in caramel, and pumpkin donuts to eat with apple cider. Desi popped one of the donuts in her mouth.

"Hey, those are for the guests." I laughed and ate one too.

"I'm just doing a quality check." She brushed a crumb off of her lips. "Do you think they're about done in there? I need to get home to my kids. Tomàs is working until midnight tonight, so Mom and Dad are watching them at my house."

I looked around. "I think we're done in here. Let's check in with Angela and Adam and see how they're doing."

We got back to the main room of the Boathouse, but they weren't where we'd left them.

"Adam? Angela?" I called.

Desi ducked her head down a few of the pathways in the haunted house. "I don't see them."

"The music is off, so they should be able to hear us." I looked around. All of the supplies had been put back where they belonged. "Maybe they went outside for some reason?"

"I guess. Adam mentioned taking out the garbage when he was done," Desi said.

A loud crashing came from the direction of the farmhouse scene. Desi and I looked at each other.

"What was that?" she whispered.

"I don't know," I whispered back. "Do you think one of them went back there?"

"What if some of the scenery fell on one of them?" She peered into the dark corridors of the haunted house.

Visions of lawsuits ran through my head. If Angela was hurt, she'd sue us for sure. I ran down the pathways in the direction of where the noise had come from. Desi followed close on my heels.

I stopped short in front of the farmhouse kitchen scene and Desi crashed into me.

"Wh—?" she started to ask, but then stopped when she saw what I was looking at.

Angela lay on the floor with her hands and feet bound and a wad of cotton stuffed in her mouth that looked suspiciously like it was from one of the zombie costumes. Blood poured from a gash in her head and she wasn't moving.

My eyes widened. What had happened to her?

"Is she dead?" Desi asked.

"I don't know." At the very least, Angela was unconscious. At the most, she was ... well, I didn't want to think about that.

"Jill!" Desi said urgently, tugging at my arm. "I saw her breathing."

I let out the air in my lungs that I didn't know I'd been holding. Thank goodness.

"We've got to get her out of here." I moved toward her, scanning the kitchen props for something to free Angela from the ropes. I didn't have a plan for moving an unconscious woman yet, but cutting the ties came first.

Desi picked up a knife from the kitchen counter. It wobbled in the air. "They're all fake."

"Yeah, think of the liability we'd have if we used real knives in the haunted house." I glanced down at Angela. "Although at this point, I'd gladly take on that risk."

We heard footsteps and rolling wheels behind us. I crossed my fingers that it was Adam looking for us and not whoever had tied up Angela.

"Hide!" Desi said. We scurried around the back of the scenery.

"I hate leaving her out there," I said under my breath.

She held up a finger to her mouth and hissed, "Shh."

Through a crack in the boards, we watched as Angela's husband, Drew, approached the farmhouse kitchen, pulling a cart that I knew Adam's crew had used when they were building the sets.

Desi and I looked at each. "Drew?" she mouthed. I nodded.

He dragged Angela onto the cart. She still didn't wake up.

The movement stirred up some construction dust and I sneezed.

He stopped and cocked his head to the side, listening.

Before Desi and I could react, he'd rounded the corner and was standing in front of where we crouched on the floor. I instinctively moved backward, closer to Desi, as if he were a mountain lion and making ourselves appear bigger would help.

He sighed. "You weren't supposed to be here."

We were too scared to say anything.

He waved a knife at us that didn't look like it was made of rubber. "Come out here so I can figure out what to do with you."

Desi and I complied. All the while, I was trying to figure out an escape plan. I knew the farmhouse kitchen was on a dead end in the haunted house, so there wasn't any other way out than the way we'd come in. I didn't want to call out for help for fear that Adam could be caught in the same trap. A ribbon of fear shot through me. What if Adam was laying helpless somewhere else in the maze? We had to get out of there.

Reluctantly, we followed him back to the farmhouse kitchen. While the haunted house was in full swing, it was frightening, but now, with only a soft glow trickling in to this scene from the overhead lights, it was terrifying—especially when a madman was waving a knife at us. My eyes darted around, looking for a means of escape, but the only way out was past Drew.

Desi held her hands up in the air. "Just let us go—we won't tell anyone."

"Right. You're as dumb as those other MUM bimbos that Angela likes to order around," he sneered at her.

She opened her mouth to say something, but I jabbed her in the side.

"Why did you tie Angela up?" I asked.

He cast a disparaging glance at his wife. "She knew too

much. I told you that she was always sticking her nose into everything. She found out this morning that Mindy and I were having an affair."

That explained why Angela seemed so down today, but what about Mindy?

"But you killed Mindy?" This wasn't making much sense. Why would he have killed his lover?

He sighed. "Mindy wanted me to break things off with Angela. Which I gladly would have done, but everything we owned was tied up in Angela's trust—the house, the art, the antiques—everything. If I left her I'd get nothing."

"Ok," I said slowly. "But then why is Angela tied up now if she already knew?"

"After she put the pieces together today about my affair with Mindy, she told me she wanted a divorce. It caught me off-guard and I wasn't sure how to proceed. But now I do." He glanced down at Angela with a gleam in his eyes. "With our prenuptial agreement, I'd lose everything, but if she dies, I'll inherit everything and nobody will be the wiser."

Now I knew why Desi's muddy footprints at Ella's birthday party had stayed on my mind. When I'd first arrived at Angela and Drew's house the day that Mindy died, his shoes had been wet. If he'd been telling the truth about not having left the house that day, they would have been dry. Instead, they'd squished down the steps when he'd directed me to the shed.

"Was Angela really embezzling from the MUMs groups?" Desi asked, staring down at Angela's prone body.

He laughed. "Not that I know of."

"So where did the forty thousand dollars come from that we found in her office?"

He sneered at Angela again. "She was always paranoid about keeping all of her money in the bank, so she kept some of it in the house, in case of emergencies. When you two discovered it, I knew it was my chance to point a finger at her for Mindy's murder. She'd told me all about your past sleuthing efforts and I knew you wouldn't be able to resist hunting for more clues about Angela's embezzlement."

My mind was reeling. He'd used us to cast blame on his wife to hide his involvement in the murder. It was a smart move, but it made me mad.

Apparently, it did the same for Desi.

"You used us?" She stared at him with fire in her eyes and took a step forward.

"Uh uh." He jabbed the knife in her direction. "Stay right there." He looked at me. "You too. Don't get any bright ideas."

I took a step back. "Ok, ok." How were we going to get out of this? An idea came to me, but I needed a little time to put it into action. I reached into the deep side pocket of my overalls and retrieved a Kleenex. Dabbing my nose, I asked, "What do you plan to do with us?"

He moved the cart with Angela in it, as if contemplating how he'd get all three of us out of there without anyone noticing.

"Just shut up. I'm thinking." His gaze darted around the farmhouse kitchen.

He didn't find any weapons either. Desi kept looking at me, her eyes widening, as if to ask me if I had any idea how to get out of this mess. While his back was turned, I winked at her. She smiled almost imperceptibly.

"I guess we're going to have to do this the hard way." He grabbed twine out of his pocket and motioned for Desi to kneel and hold her hands out to him.

Desi looked at me and I nodded. "Do what he says."

Drew looked up at me. "Good girl. This will be easier for all of us if you do what I say."

He bent down to tie her wrists, putting the knife down just beyond her reach. While he was distracted, I reached into my pocket again and touched a button. Within a few seconds, a machine kicked on. Drew looked at me.

I shrugged. "It's an old building with a loud furnace."

He returned to tying Desi's hands and feet, while still keeping an eye on me.

Thick gray fog shot out from behind the refrigerator façade in the farmhouse kitchen, swirling around Drew and Desi.

"What the ...?" He leaned back, coughing. He fumbled in his coat pocket for something. "Did you do that? Turn it off. I'm asthma—"

The rest of his sentence was interrupted by another coughing fit, this time racking his whole body as he fought to breathe. Desi scooted away from him, kicking the knife toward me. I quickly cut through her bindings and we backed away.

We hurried around Drew and I grabbed the cart handle, dragging Angela out of the direct path of the fog. I was pretty sure it wouldn't hurt her, but better safe than sorry. From behind us, I heard a noise, followed quickly by a welcome sight—Adam.

"I heard him threatening you. Are you ok?" He put his arms on my shoulders and looked me up and down. "I've called the police. They should be here any minute."

I nodded.

"I'm fine, too, thanks for asking," Desi said, mock glaring at her brother.

He sighed and was about to say something back to her, but he noticed Drew on the floor sucking on his inhaler.

The fog continued to assail him, rendering him a coughing mess on the floor.

"Here," I said, handing Adam some twine from the floor. "Use this."

He grabbed Drew's feet and then his hands, tying them together but allowing enough range of motion for him to continue to use his inhaler.

"I think you can turn it off now," he said.

I reached in my pocket and hit the off button on the fog machine's controller.

The fog dissipated quickly. With the machine turned off, the sound of police sirens was apparent.

"I'll go get them," Desi volunteered. She returned a minute later with four police officers in tow.

"She needs medical attention." I pointed to Angela, still unconscious in the cart. "Her husband hit her over the head with something."

The police office called for an ambulance. When the EMTs arrived, they rushed Angela away to the hospital. Another ambulance came for Drew, who was still suffering the aftereffects of the fog machine.

When everyone finally left, I checked my cell phone. I had several frantic messages from my parents wondering where I was. I called them back to let them know we'd had an emergency situation at the Boathouse but that we were all ok.

When I hung up, Adam was standing next to me.

"What happened to Angela? Where were you?" I asked. "I was so worried."

He sighed. "I took the trash out to the dumpster, but the dumb lid was stuck and I had to pry it open. It took me longer than usual and when I returned I heard voices in the haunted house. That's when I found you." He put his arms around me and pulled me close. "I've never been so scared in my life. How do you and Desi keep getting yourselves involved in these situations?"

I shook my head. "I don't know. They just seem to happen. Maybe the event planning business is more dangerous than you'd think."

He pressed his lips together and eyed me as though he was about to object. Instead, he just kissed me and held me close. By this time, Tomàs had arrived and I could see Desi receiving the same lecture. This had definitely not been the perfect opening night I'd hoped for.

22

"With any luck, this night will go better than last night," Desi said. We were both watching as each person in line entered the haunted house. "They look like they're enjoying it."

I nodded. "I don't think it could get much worse."

As soon as I said that, Nancy Davenport came into view. I ducked behind the counter in the lobby. "I take that back."

Desi laughed at me. "Still scared of the wicked witch?"

"Haha." I looked up at her. "Is she gone yet?"

"Yes. She just went in. You're safe for a few more minutes."

I groaned. If only she could get lost inside the haunted house.

"I'll go find Adam. I'm sure he'll want to show her the kids' section of the haunted house." She probably wouldn't approve of it, but at least he'd tried.

"Anthony said it was awesome," Desi said. "His words, not mine."

"Mikey too. Adam somehow made it scary enough but not too scary for little kids." In all the years we'd been married, I'd never known Adam had such a creative side, but it had really shown through on this project. I'd have to keep it in mind when Mikey came home with all of the projects I knew he'd have when he entered elementary school the next year.

I located Adam and we waited outside on the dock for Nancy to exit the haunted house. She came out alongside her husband and youngest daughter. All of them were smiling. Whoa. Something had actually made Nancy Davenport smile. Had Adam put laughing gas in there today?

Nancy spotted Adam and me standing there and came over to us.

"Adam, that was great. I loved it. I'm so glad you took my suggestion to make a kids' section." She looked at me pointedly. "Jill said that you wouldn't be able to do it this year, but you must be more efficient than her."

I bit my tongue, but I could feel the anger rising up in my chest, threatening to spill over.

Adam smiled graciously. "Thank you." He put his arms on my shoulders and started to lead me away. "Jill and I had better get going now. There's so much that goes on behind the scenes here."

He guided me back to my office. "Better?"

I nodded. "She really gets to me."

He shrugged. "Nancy does seem to hate you for some reason. What did you do to her?"

"Nothing! I swear." I sighed. "She's just a mean witch."

"Well, you're going to have to figure out a way to work with her. Mikey will be at that school for another year and, in a few years, Ella might go there. It's a waste of energy to fight with her for that long."

I stared at him. He was probably right, but I didn't know if I was ready to give in to Nancy and play nice.

"I'll make an effort to be nice to Nancy."

"Great. Now really, we have work to do." He grabbed my hand and I followed him back to the haunted house.

~

"Oh my gosh," Desi said. "Aren't they just the most adorable things you've ever seen?"

I laughed. We'd hung back at the street and allowed Mikey and Anthony to go up to a house to trick-or-treat on their own. The boys were standing on someone's front porch in their Halloween costumes, holding out their fat plastic pumpkins so the man at the door could dump candy in the opening. Their eyes were wide as he gave them each four pieces of candy and they thanked him profusely.

Adam and Tomàs stood next to us. My husband wore his Luke costume and he'd convinced me to wear the Leia outfit, so for the first time in a long time, I was wearing a costume on Halloween. I had to admit, it was actually rather fun and I felt like I was a part of the whole Halloween celebration.

Angela, Beth, and Lincoln were running the haunted house on its last night so that I'd be free to go trick-or-treating with the kids. Angela and I were never going to be best friends, but if Beth decided to offer up the Boathouse for the event next year, I had a feeling that things would go better between us. She'd even begrudgingly complimented Adam on his creepy farm designs and asked him if he'd be willing to help with it next year. The state had enough evidence in Mindy's murder to put Drew away for a long time, and I think she was a little lonely in that big house by herself, because she'd invited our MUMs group for a holiday tea at the end of November.

It seemed crazy to think that Thanksgiving and Christmas would be upon us before we knew it. While Halloween was Adam's favorite holiday, I loved how Christmas seemed to bring families together. What I didn't love was the stress that came along with it. Beth and I had sat down yesterday to finalize the Boathouse's calendar for mid-November through the end of the year and we were booked solid for almost every weeknight and completely sold out for the weekends. I wouldn't have much time to hang out in front of the Christmas tree eating cookies this year, but on my days off, I planned to make up for lost time by hanging out with Adam and the kids. Nothing was more important than my family.

"Hey," Desi said, cutting into my daydream about Christmas trees and cookies. "Did Mom tell you that Will and his family are coming to visit for Christmas this year?"

"No, she didn't mention it." Will was Adam's older brother and I hadn't seen him in a few years. He and his wife lived in Phoenix, and due to his job as an in-demand dermatologist, they weren't able to come and visit their parents much, much to my mother-in-law's dismay.

"Hmm. She must have forgotten to tell you. I think she spoke to Adam about it."

"Maybe." I glanced at Adam. He was reaching for Mikey's hand to help him cross the street to the next row of houses.

"I told Will that you'd be happy to have them stay with you while they're here. We just don't have room for them at our house." She laughed. "Much as I love our old house, it just isn't that big."

I froze. "What?" Will and his wife Tania were rather standoffish and they had three obnoxious kids. My house went through enough having a four-year-old boy living there; I didn't think there'd be a house left standing if Will and his family came to stay. "I thought they usually stayed with your parents." I held my breath. I knew they were Adam's family, but I really didn't want them staying with us.

"They're having their house painted in December, remember? Tania can't be around paint fumes. She says they make her head hurt."

"Oh." I stared at Adam and Tomàs, who were now a few houses away, down the street. "I guess that would be ok."

Desi broke out into laughter. "Gotcha!"

My eyes drilled into her face. "What?"

"I'm joking. They're coming to visit, but they'll stay with Mom and Dad."

"What about the painting?"

"Oh they're going to put that off until January." She laughed again. "You should have seen your face."

"Desi!" I slugged her arm. "That was mean."

"Hey, that's my brother you're talking about." She danced away from me down the sidewalk.

Immediately, I felt bad. "I just mean ..."

"That his kids are horrible?" She gave me an impish grin. "I'm in complete agreement. But they're my nieces and I still love them. Besides, it's been a few years since I've seen them. Maybe they've improved."

"Maybe." I remembered meeting the three girls for the first time when Mikey was a baby. I'd had to keep them from trampling him and had spent the entire dinner at my in-laws' house being terrified they'd do something to him. "Anyway, it will be nice for them to visit at Christmas this year."

Desi nodded. "Mom's trying to convince Sarah to come up here too."

"I haven't seen her in years." Both of Adam's other

siblings lived too far away for frequent visits, and with two little kids, we hadn't made a strong effort to visit them either. I glanced at the kids in their costumes. It was hard to believe it would be Christmas in less than two months. "I love Ericksville at Christmas. The decorated tree in Lighthouse Park, the pretty lights they put up downtown—everything."

"Me too."

We both looked over at the kids, so happy with their dads.

"Don't you just want to soak it in sometimes?" Desi asked. "They'll be over the whole trick-or-treating thing before we know it."

"I know." I looked over at Mikey, who was fooling around with his cousin. "I'm always reminded of that saying, 'the days are long but the years are short.' They may be little stinkers sometimes, but we just need to enjoy them while they still want us around."

"Yep," Desi said. "I try to remind myself of that when Anthony throws a tantrum about putting his shoes on."

Adam and Tomàs came over to us with the boys.

"I think they're ready to call it quits," Tomàs said. Both boys were dragging a little and I wondered if we'd make it home before they collapsed.

Adam and I said goodbye to Desi and family, and they turned off toward their house while we walked up the hill toward ours.

"I think that went well," Adam said happily.

"We survived Halloween and the haunted house." I suddenly felt better about everything. This last month had been tough, but now I had Christmas to look forward to and nothing was going to spoil that for me.

~

Thank you for reading Murderous Mummy Wars. I hope you enjoyed spending more time with Jill Andrews and her family. If you did, I'd really appreciate it if you left a review.

For information about my new releases and other exciting news, please visit my website, nicoleellisauthor.com and sign up for my e-mail newsletter.

~

BOOKS BY NICOLE ELLIS

Jill Andrews Cozy Mysteries
Brownie Points for Murder - Book #1
Death to the Highest Bidder - Book #2
A Deadly Pair O'Docks - Book #3
Stuck with S'More Death - Book #4

Candle Beach Sweet Romances
Sweet Beginnings - Book #1
Sweet Success - Book #2
Sweet Promises - Book #3
Sweet Memories - Book #4
Sweet History - Book #5

<<<<>>>>

Made in the USA
San Bernardino, CA
26 July 2019